]

House

by

Kathi Daley

This book is a work of fiction. Names, characters, places, and incidents either are products of the author's imagination or are used fictitiously. Any resemblance to actual events or locales or persons, living or dead, is entirely coincidental.

Copyright © 2018 by Katherine Daley

Version 1.0

All rights reserved, including the right of reproduction in whole or in part in any form.

I want to thank the very talented Jessica Fischer for the cover art.

I so appreciate Bruce Curran, who is always ready and willing to answer my cyber questions; Jayme Maness for helping out with the book clubs; and Peggy Hyndman for helping sleuth out those pesky typos.

Special thanks to Joyce Aiken, Sharon Guagliardo, Patty Liu, and Vivian Shane for submitting recipes.

And, of course, thanks to the readers and bloggers in my life, who make doing what I do possible.

Thank you to Randy Ladenheim-Gil for the editing.

And finally, I want to thank my husband Ken for allowing me time to write by taking care of everything else.

Chapter 1

Monday, October 22

The thing that hit me hardest as I stood in a dark, dank basement struggling to make sense of a death by vampire less than two weeks before Halloween, was that someone had gone to a lot of trouble to put this whole thing together. A stormy night, a creepy old house, a dog in peril, a body in the basement, and a legendary killer who couldn't possibly be real.

"Walk me through everything that happened from the beginning," Sheriff Salinger, a nemesis turned friend, said to me after he'd covered the body with a white sheet while we waited for the coroner.

I reached up to wipe a spiderweb from my hair before I began to speak. "I was at the Zoo." I referred to Zoe's Zoo, the wild and domestic animal rescue and rehabilitation shelter I owned. "I was about to close up when I got a call about a barking dog that was reportedly trapped inside an abandoned house. Jeremy usually closes up at five, but he was off today.

He'd volunteered to chaperone his daughter Morgan's preschool field trip to the pumpkin patch. I remembered doing that when I was a kid. So fun."

"I don't think I need quite that much detail," Salinger said.

"You're right. I'm sorry. The point is, not only was Jeremy off today but it also happens to be Monday. Aspen's started working Saturdays so we can offer adoption services six days a week. Because she works Saturdays, Aspen has begun to take Mondays off." I could see Salinger was becoming impatient with the details of the lives of my employees, Jeremy Fisher and Aspen Wood, but this part was important. "So not only were Jeremy and Aspen not available to take the call, but my third in command, Tiffany Middlcton, who recently married Scott Walden, the veterinarian, has decided she only wants to work half days. She gets off at two." I paused, giving Salinger time to catch up. "I'm sure you can see where I'm going with this."

"I have no idea where you're going with this," Salinger countered.

I paused as a clap of thunder shook the old wooden structure. If I hadn't been so terrified, I would admire the artistry of it all. I wondered if the storm was just a coincidence, or if whoever put this thing together intentionally waited for one to roll in. I cringed as a second clap of thunder followed the first, then returned my attention to the sheriff. "On almost any other day, there would have been someone else at the Zoo to respond to a routine barking dog call. Someone other than me. The fact that this place," I swept my hand around the room, "is arranged exactly the way it is tells me that whoever killed this man wanted me, and only me, to find the body."

Salinger still looked confused, although I thought I was being quite clear. "Don't you see?" I continued. "A creepy old house, a dog in peril, and a body in the basement. Doesn't it seem just a tiny bit familiar?"

Salinger rubbed his chin with his right hand, as if trying to work through the details with which he'd been presented. After a moment he spoke. "The scene does seem familiar."

"The setup is the same as the scene I found when I stumbled upon the body of Coach Griswold five years ago. The way this body is posed is even the same, although the method of death is most decidedly different."

Salinger bent down for a closer look. He gently lifted the sheet, took a closer look at the victim, and then looked back at me. "So we have a copycat."

"Perhaps. But if I recall correctly, you and I are the only two people to have witnessed the scene of the first crime. I know I didn't set this up so…" I raised a brow at Salinger.

"Of course I didn't do it," Salinger huffed. "The details of Coach Griswold's death are in the file. Photos and such. I suppose they could have been leaked at some point. It happens. But my real question is, if someone wanted to get your attention, why did they duplicate that murder? You've been involved in dozens of murder investigations over the years, so why this particular murder out of all the possibilities?"

"I don't know. I hate the idea that a man is dead and it could very well be my fault indirectly, but I really do feel it's possible all this has been arranged for my benefit."

"You think this man was murdered as a prop for whatever sick game someone is playing with you?"

I shrugged. "Maybe. I hope not, but everything about the scene of this murder seems too perfect not to have been intentional. The call about the dog was made anonymously. The person I spoke to said they didn't want to leave a name, but they felt they should call because they were afraid the dog was trapped inside the house. I was the one to respond because I was the only one at the Zoo. When I got here there was a dog in the house, tied up in the basement. I guess whoever set this up wanted to be sure I'd check the basement."

Salinger stood up and took out a notepad. "Where is this dog now?"

"In my car, with Charlie. I didn't want the dogs to have to wait down here with the body." I glanced at the sheet on the floor. "Who do you think it is?"

Salinger shook his head. "I don't know. The victim doesn't have identification on him. I'll run his prints after we get him to the morgue." Salinger used his flashlight to look around the room. The storm had totally blotted out any light that would have been provided by the late afternoon sun, and the only window was a small area of glass high on the wall, at ground level from the outside. "So, if this little murder scene was set up for your benefit do you have any idea *who* might have done it? Any idea at all?"

"Well, my first thought, given the fact that the man seems to have died from a bite to the neck, is Dracula, although I suppose it could have been another vampire altogether."

"Dracula didn't kill this man. A vampire didn't kill this man."

"How do you know?" I asked with a slight lilt to my voice.

Salinger glanced at me. "Dracula isn't real. Vampires aren't real."

I raised a brow. "Then how do you explain the two little puncture wounds in the man's neck? I've watched my share of vampire movies. I know what I'm looking at. Maybe someone I helped send to jail was turned and has come back to enact his revenge."

Salinger chuckled. *"Enact his revenge.* That's precious. While I love your childlike belief in possibilities, I can assure you, a living person killed this man, not an undead creature of the night."

I crossed my arms over my chest. "Okay, then, if not a vampire, who?"

"I don't know. Yet," Salinger said.

I could hear more thunder rolling in from the distance. Charlie wasn't normally the sort to cower when we had lightning storms, but he'd been left in the car with a strange dog after witnessing me have a bit of a freak out when I found the body. I should wrap this up and go check on him.

"You said it seemed the stage had been set for your benefit," Salinger said. "Say that's true. Does anyone come to mind who might be motivated to do all this? Anyone human?"

I let out a little half laugh. "I'll admit that as I was driving out here with the rain pouring down all around my car, I thought it might have been Zak who'd sent me on this fateful mission," I said, referring to my husband, Zak Zimmerman.

Salinger dropped his jaw. "Why on earth would Zak kill a man and then stage this scene for you?"

"Oh, he wouldn't," I quickly answered. "It was just that after I got the barking dog call and realized the dog that was overheard seemed to be trapped in the Henderson House, I remembered I'd received the same call five years ago. As I made my way out here in the middle of a rainstorm, it occurred to me that my very caring and inventive husband might have set up a surprise to try to lure me out of my funk. Not that he would lure me with a dead body, mind you. I didn't know we were dealing with an actual murder until after I got here. But as I made the trip out, it occurred to me that maybe Zak had arranged for me to respond to the same call I did years ago to bring some Halloween fun into my life."

"You suspected Zak would send you to a house where you previously found a dead body as a prank?"

"Not a prank exactly. More like a gift. I suspected that when I arrived I'd find a bunch of decorations. Maybe a mannequin mimicking a murder victim."

"I have to say, the two of you are the oddest couple."

"Not odd really," I countered. "Zak knows I usually love Halloween and appreciate a genuine scare. Normally, it wouldn't occur to me that he would go to such lengths, but I'm afraid I've been complaining to anyone who will listen that I'm having a hard time finding the magic of the holiday this year. It seemed like a Zak thing to do to scare the Halloween back into me. He's sweet that way."

Salinger chuckled again before taking out his camera. "I wouldn't be too worried about not feeling the usual magic this year," he said as he began snapping photos. "You do have a lot on your plate, and I suppose at your age the level of excitement you feel over holidays—or anything actually—fades somewhat."

I leaned a hip against the wall. "But that's just it. I don't want the fantasy to fade. Yes, I know I have a baby who requires a lot of my attention, and I'm raising two teenagers as well as seeing to Zak's adopted grandmother. I do understand that a certain level of fatigue comes with all that. But I don't want to settle into old ladyhood quite yet. I want to feel happy anticipation. I want to go crazy at the Halloween store picking out decorations, and I want to look forward to the Zoe Donovan Halloween Spooktacular rather than dreading all the extra work it's going to generate. I hate that I find myself wondering if we shouldn't have just skipped the party this year."

Salinger stopped snapping photos. He reached out and put a hand on my arm. "I understand how you feel. I feel the same way sometimes. But you have a long way to go before anyone is going to consider you old. Fatigue might be dimming your enthusiasm right now, but Catherine is getting older, and soon she won't require as much care, and Nona seems to be settling into her new situation."

I let out a sigh. "Yeah, I guess. Zak says I should try to focus on the things in my life that fit the way things are now, like finding a cute costume for Catherine rather than worrying about the fact that I don't have time to organize the zombie run this year. I know he's right. But I've never been good with change, and there have been a lot of changes in my life lately."

"I can agree that your life has undergone a lot of change in a short period of time," Salinger said. "But no matter what life throws at you, you're the most capable person I know. Give yourself a break and try to enjoy what you have instead of fretting over what you've had to give up."

I smiled. 'Thanks. That helps. Zak, Levi, and Ellie have all been saying the exact same thing, but somehow it's a bit more convincing coming from you."

Salinger took out a plastic bag and, using a gloved hand, bagged a discarded bottle cap as well as a partially smoked cigarette. "Glad I can help."

I glanced at the door leading out to the hallway. "I can hear a car in the drive."

"It must be the medical examiner. I'll need to chat with him for a while. Why don't you go on home to that family of yours? I think it would be best if you stayed close to home until we get this figured out."

I nodded. "Will you call me when you know whose body this is?"

"I will. I'm hoping we know by evening, but if not, maybe tomorrow morning. Of course, if the man's prints aren't in the system, our job is going to be a whole lot harder. He doesn't look at all familiar to me, so I don't think he's a local. He could just be someone passing through. If I don't get a hit from the fingerprints and he doesn't match any missing persons reports, I'll start looking at the lodging properties in the area."

"If I can help let me know."

"You can't. You're retired from the sleuthing game. Remember?"

I nodded. "I remember. That's just another change I'm trying to get my head around. If I don't hear from you this evening I'll talk to you tomorrow."

I left the house through the rear; the back of the house was the closest to the basement, and suddenly, I felt claustrophobic. It was still raining, but getting wet seemed preferable to spending even one more minute in the stale air that had been trapped inside. I stepped from the small porch into the yard behind the house, turned, and looked back. I knew from previous visits that the structure was two stories, plus the attic and basement. It sat toward the back of a large, overgrown lot surrounded by an iron fence and an impenetrable gate that opened onto a dirt drive leading to a walkway comprised of four rotted steps and an equally rotted porch. The house, once owned by Hezekiah Henderson, certainly had seen more than its share of death.

Hezekiah was already an old man when I was a child. A *crazy* old man, I'd like to add. Although he'd seemed to have adequate financial resources, he'd chosen to live as a recluse who rarely, if ever, left his creepy old house. When I was seven, one of my classmates told me that in his youth, Hezekiah had murdered and then dismembered over a hundred people. It was rumored he'd buried the body parts under the floorboards in the basement and then settled into a life of seclusion to maintain the spell he'd used to trap the souls of his victims in limbo for all time. Of course, I didn't necessarily believe the story to be true, but, like I said, the house had seen more than its share of death. Hezekiah died when I was nine, and for years after that, no one dared enter the creepy place, though as time went by the rumors ceased, and vagrants began to use the building to ward off cold winter nights. The legend of Hezekiah Henderson and the haunted basement faded.

Then, seventeen years ago, a bunch of counselors from a nearby summer camp decided to have a party in the old house. Before the night was over, four counselors were dead. Which brings us to five years ago, when I found Coach Griswold's body in the basement. That murder had had a very human explanation, but that didn't stop a ghost hunter from coming to town four years ago to research paranormal activity in the house. He seemed to be on to some sort of a revelation until his body was found at the bottom of the stairs a few days later.

When I returned to my car my best little pal and constant sidekick, Charlie, was waiting impatiently with the very pregnant cocker spaniel I'd rescued from the house. "I'm sorry it took so long." I grabbed a towel from the back seat and dried my face and hair. "I knew you'd be worried, but having you both wait in the car seemed the best course of action." I looked at the spaniel. "So, what are we going to do with you?" The dog cowered on the back seat, which I guess I understood. The poor thing had probably been dognapped, then tied up in the basement of Henderson House for who knew how long. "I guess I'll take you home until we can find your humans. It looks like those pups could come at any time, and it will be much more comforting to be around people than to be locked up in a pen at the Zoo."

Fortunately, the Zimmerman clan was between fosters. In addition to Charlie, we had two full-time dogs and three full-time cats. More often than not, we also had a dog, a cat, or both, we were fostering.

Currently, however, the spare room was free of any temporary furry guests. I called the house and spoke to Alex, the fourteen-year-old girl who lived with Zak and me. I told her what had happened and that I was on my way, and she agreed to start dinner. Scooter, the fourteen-year-old boy who lived with us too, had soccer practice after school, which had been moved to the gymnasium due to the rain. That was where Zak would be picking him up. I was fairly certain both would be home shortly. I'd left my almost-ten-month-old daughter with my best friend, Ellie Denton, so I'd need to stop at the boathouse where she lived with her husband Levi and toddler Eli, before heading home for the evening.

Charlie settled in the front seat and the mama spaniel curled up with the blanket I'd found in my trunk in the back, and I started the car and drove slowly down the rutted dirt road. The pouring rain had created large puddles that I navigated carefully so as not to jostle my pregnant passenger any more than I had to. While the rain was still coming down, it seemed the thunder and lightning had moved on, at least for now. The sky was still heavy with dark clouds, so I had no doubt another round of thunderstorms could be in our future.

The rain had caused minor flooding in low-lying areas, so I took it slow once I reached pavement as well. I turned on the radio to the easy listening station in an effort to provide a distraction from my thoughts, and to introduce a calming element to the overall atmosphere of the vehicle. I felt tense, and if I was tense, Charlie would be too, and the poor mama spaniel looked scared to death.

A few minutes later, I glanced in the rearview mirror to the seat behind me. It appeared the spaniel had gone to sleep. I didn't blame her a bit. The whole ordeal must have been very trying for a mama so far along in her pregnancy. I'd need to put Catherine in the back seat once I picked her up, so I decided to run by the house, drop off the dogs with Alex, then head over to the boathouse to pick up my baby.

******

"You found another body in Henderson House?" Ellie asked after I'd greeted Catherine, who was sitting on the floor playing with Eli. Or at least playing near him. It didn't seem as if she necessarily cared whether he joined in or not. "Doesn't that make three bodies you've found in that house?"

"I didn't technically find the parapsychologist who died four years ago, so in terms of bodies I've found in the house, this only makes two. This is the third murder that's taken place in that house in the past five years, however."

"Someone should just tear that place down. The number of people who have died in that house over the years is ridiculous. I'm not one to be superstitious, but I'd almost be willing to bet the place is cursed. Do you know who this victim is?"

I shook my head, raising my lips on one side in a sort of half grin. "I didn't recognize him, but I can tell you that the killer was a vampire."

Ellie lifted both brows. "A vampire?"

"The guy had these two little holes in his neck that looked exactly like a vampire bite."

"You know vampires aren't real."

I lifted one shoulder, enjoying the look of disbelief on Ellie's face. "Maybe."

She began to catch onto my game and rolled her eyes. "Why would someone make a murder look like a vampire attack? It feels weird and intentional."

"It *was* weird and intentional." I went on to explain my theory that the killer had specifically intended for me to be the one who found the body. I shared my thoughts about the dog being tied up in the basement and the call to the Zoo when I would be the only one there.

"So you think you were lured there?" Ellie gasped. "That terrifies me."

I bit my lower lip, a more serious mood overtaking me. "Yeah. The fact that the scene seemed to have been set for my benefit is bothering me as well."

"You don't think it was Claudia…?" Ellie asked.

Claudia Lotherman was a woman I suppose could be classified as my archnemesis. Not only had she tried to kill me twice in the last several years but she'd kidnapped Zak the previous spring and made me pass a bunch of tests to get him back. The last I heard, she was still in the wind and no one knew exactly where she'd holed up, but I had a hard time believing she'd come back to Ashton Falls when so many people were looking for her. Still, she *had* concocted an elaborate scheme when she kidnapped Zak.

"I suppose it's possible Claudia is behind this," I agreed. "The vampire thing seems like something she'd do, and she's a master of disguise, so she might be able to slip into town unnoticed. But it seems like a huge risk for her to come back here so soon after her last visit, so I'm thinking it isn't her, even if she is a total loon. So, maybe. I'll mention it to Salinger when he calls later and see what he thinks."

"If the person who killed that man and left him for you to find wasn't Claudia, then who?" Ellie asked. "With everything you've told me it really does sound like you're being targeted. Someone really seems to want to mess with you. We know Claudia will go to great lengths just to yank your chain, but other than her, I can't think of a single person who would go to so much trouble. I mean really, a vampire? Who would do such a thing?"

I wished I knew. The idea that someone had set up the murder for my benefit bothered me quite a lot. I had to wonder if the body I'd found in the basement was the beginning and the end to whatever was going to happen, or if there were other people at risk of being killed just so someone could get at me. I'd been struggling with that idea ever since I'd found the body, that perhaps I was the reason a man had died on this blustery day in late October. I just couldn't figure out how anyone could possibly know the details of that first death all those years ago.

"Do you need me to watch Catherine tomorrow?" Ellie asked when I didn't speak for a couple of minutes.

"No," I answered, pulling myself out of my thoughts and into the present. "I plan to be home. Do you want to come over? We can work on a menu for the Halloween Spooktacular. I'd like to do theme foods, the way we have in the past, and of course we'll need chicken wings for Levi. But I thought we could add some new things as well. Maybe we can throw in a few more desserts. I bought a Halloween recipe book when I went to the market last week. I bet we can find some ideas in it that haven't occurred to us before."

"I'd love to come by your place for a visit, and I do want to go over the menu, but I have a doctor's appointment in the morning, so it'll have to be in the afternoon."

"Is everything okay?" I asked. Ellie was pregnant with child number two.

"Everything is perfect, although I'm a little nervous. Tomorrow is the day I finally find out the sex of the baby."

I smiled. "That's great. I've been dying to know. I don't know why you waited so long to have the ultrasound."

Ellie let out a breath. "I guess I was scared, so I procrastinated."

I narrowed my gaze. "Scared? Why? Because you're hoping for a girl and will be disappointed if it's a boy, or do you want another boy and will be let down if it's a girl?"

"Exactly."

"To which one?" I asked.

"Both."

Chapter 2

Later that evening, I sat at the dinner table with Zak, Zak's honorary grandmother, Nona, Alex, Scooter, and, of course, baby Catherine. The pregnant mama dog had taken to Alex, who I knew was an excellent foster mother, so we set her up in her room. Charlie was lounging nearby with the other Zimmerman canines, Bella and Digger, while the family cats were all curled up on the sofa in the living room.

"I think I've figured out what I want to dress up as for the Halloween dance Zimmerman Academy is having on Saturday," Alex said.

"Oh, and what's that?" I asked.

"Marie Curie. Diego is going to go as Pierre Curie. We thought it would be fun to do a couple's costume, and we wanted to do someone from history. We're going to wear lab coats, and I'm going to wear my hair up the way she has it in a lot of photos. We figured we'd wear name badges because the costumes won't be totally obvious, the way a ghost or witch costume would be."

I glanced at Zak, waiting for him to blow a gasket, but instead he just smiled and said he couldn't wait to see how the outfits came out. Okay, this was good. I guess that meant he was getting used to Alex and Diego as a couple. He hadn't been thrilled at first, but personally, I really liked Diego, and if Alex was going to date, I wanted her to date a responsible and caring person like him. Besides, he'd helped me save Zak's life when Claudia had kidnapped him, so as far as I was concerned, he'd passed any sort of concerned-mama test I could throw at him.

"I'm going to be a ninja," Scooter said after a beat.

"Weren't you a ninja last year?" I asked as I forked up a piece of potato.

"No. Last year I was a samurai. It's totally different."

I wasn't an expert, but they seemed pretty much the same to me. Still, if Scooter wanted to be a ninja for Halloween that was fine, as long as he was happy with his choice. I knew he would be attending his first boy/girl dance at the public school he attended and I wanted him to have a wonderful time despite the fact that he planned to attend with his best friend Tucker instead of taking a date.

"What's Catherine going to be?" Scooter asked.

"I'm not sure yet," I answered. "I guess I should head into town and choose something before everything is picked over. Did you ask Tucker about the Halloween party here at the house?"

"He's coming," Scooter said.

"Diego too," Alex seconded.

When I first began having my now-famous Halloween parties they were strictly an adult affair, but now that most of our friends had children, we'd changed things up a bit to make it a family event. My parents planned to attend with my four-year-old sister Harper, Jeremy was bringing his three daughters, and Levi and Ellie would be bringing Eli. My mom's friend Ava said she'd stop by with her two children, so I imagined we'd have eleven or twelve kids ten and under, in addition to the ten or twelve teens I knew were planning to show. Of course, I'd also invited everyone from my senior book group, so the over-sixty crowd would be represented as well.

"Are you planning to dress up?" I asked Nona.

"I thought I'd come as a biker chick. I can't ride my bike much, but I still have the jacket, leather pants, and boots. I'm not sure yet what I'm going to do about a date. I'll let you know if I decide to bring someone."

Before her brain tumor and surgery, Nona had ridden a pink Harley, but since recovering, she seemed to have tamed the wild woman she had once been. In her place was a very nice and mostly responsible grandmotherly type. I missed Nona the hell-raiser, who seemed to have lived without filters of any kind, but I knew the life she lived now was not only better for her health but a lot more compatible with living in a family unit. Still, I wondered if crazy Nona would suddenly appear again one day.

I turned and looked at Zak. "I noticed you finished decorating the entry. The garland on the staircase looks really nice. Are we done with the interior of the house?"

"Almost," Zak, who tended to go just a bit crazy with the decorations every holiday season, answered. "I want to do a display in the entry, and I'm still thinking of adding something to the garden window in the kitchen. I do, however, plan to commit most of my time and effort to finishing the outside decorations. I'm behind this year."

"When are you going to put up Mr. and Mrs. Frankenstein?" Scooter asked Zak. "They're my favorites."

"I guess I can do them tomorrow. You don't have soccer and I don't have any meetings or anything after school. Do you want to help?"

Scooter grinned and nodded. "Maybe we should add a baby Frankenstein this year because we have baby Catherine."

"And two teenage Frankensteins, because you have us," Alex added.

"If I can find two teens and a baby we'll make them be part of the display," Zak promised. "Do you want to help Scooter and me?" Zak asked Alex.

"I would, but I'm going to the library to work on my history project with Hazel. Grandpa said he'd come by to help out too." Hazel Hampton, now Hazel Donovan since marrying my grandpa, was the town librarian.

"What are you researching?" I wondered.

"The Norlander mine. It's pretty interesting so far. Did you know that the Norlander brothers pulled tens of thousands of dollars' worth of gold out of that mine before they were both murdered? Some people say it was even more than that. And that was a century ago, so just think about how much money that would be now."

"I wasn't aware it was that much," I said, "although I do remember hearing it was a very profitable mine, unlike some in the area."

Alex set her fork on her plate. "Hazel said it was the most prosperous mine around when the brothers were murdered."

"Murdered?" Nona asked.

Alex nodded. "It's assumed they were killed by another miner, set on taking over their claim, but the killer was never caught and the mining operations sort of fizzled out shortly after the brothers died, so no one ever did take over. Hazel said by the time the brothers were killed, the mine was about done producing, so the really sad thing is, if the brothers were murdered for their claim, they died for nothing. Of course, the motive was never verified because the killer was never found, so I guess it's possible they were murdered for another reason altogether. Grandpa said there was probably a woman involved."

"Why would he say that?" I wondered.

"I asked him that, and he said there's always a woman involved."

"That's Grandpa for you." I laughed. "Always ready with a joke."

"Are you talking about that haunted mine up on the mountain?" Scooter asked when there was a pause in the conversation. "The one with all the fencing around it?"

Alex turned to Scooter. "Maybe. I haven't been up there and I'm not sure which mine you're talking about. There are a lot of them. But I do know it's up on the mountain, so it could be."

"I'm talking about the one with the big sign telling everyone to stay out."

I looked at Scooter and nodded. "I think the mine you're talking about is the one Alex is studying."

"You know that mine is haunted," Scooter warned her.

"There's a legend that the brothers stayed behind to protect their claim even after they both died, so I suppose it could be haunted. How do you know about the mine?" I asked.

"Some of the kids at school were talking about it. If it's the one I'm thinking of, the brothers were killed on Halloween night. Their bodies were ripped apart, like some animal got to them. A few of the guys said it was a werewolf that killed them. Others said it was just a bear. No one knows for sure, but most of the guys were pretty sure something supernatural was going on up there on the mountain."

Alex laughed. "While it's true the brothers' bodies were mutilated, the real story is that they were killed with a pickax. At least that's what I read in the old history book Hazel lent me."

I grabbed a napkin and wiped Catherine's face. "Why exactly are you researching this mine?"

"The assignment was to write a paper about a person or a place that helped to shape Ashton Fall's history. A lot of people are doing papers on people like Ashton Montgomery and places like the old medical clinic, but I wanted to do something different. Hazel said the little mining town that sprang up didn't amount to much until the Norlander brothers struck it rich. Once word got out about the piles of gold they were pulling out of the mountain, other miners came to the area, and what was once nothing more than a camp turned into an actual town. Of course, the town that grew up from the mining operation was called Devil's Den back then, but Devil's Den is part of Ashton Fall's history." Alex looked at Scooter. "And yes, the fact that the mine is reported to be haunted and that the brothers died on Halloween is an extra bonus given the time of year. I thought it would be fun to do a story with spooky undertones."

"It sounds like an interesting project," Zak said. "I'd like to read it when you're done."

"Sure, I didn't know whether the paper would come together when I first started looking into it, but Hazel has been a big help. Ethan too," Alex added, referring to another of the teachers at the Academy. "Between the two of them, they knew a lot of stories about Devil's Den. It's been tricky separating fact from fiction, given the way the brothers died, but the assignment was to write about a place, and legend is part of history, after all."

"I heard the brothers were buried up there near the mine, but when the townsfolk went up to the graves to lay flowers the day after they were buried, the ground had been dug up and the bodies were gone," Scooter informed us.

Alex frowned. "I think that must just be a story. I've been reading about the mine for a week and haven't heard anything about that. In fact, I think the brothers were buried in the old cemetery at the base of the mining camp, with everyone else who died around that time." Alex looked at me. "Have you heard anything about missing bodies?"

I shook my head. "No. But then again, it isn't like I studied the subject. I do know there have been a lot of ghost stories told over the years about what happened to the brothers."

"Zombie story," Scooter said.

"Zombie?" I asked.

"The brothers' graves were empty the day after they were buried, so they were zombies, not ghosts. That would make them zombie stories, not ghost stories."

******

After dinner the kids went up to do their homework and Nona retired to her suite to watch television. Zak offered to do the dishes while I gave Catherine her bath. We'd settled into a routine that revolved around Alex and Scooter's after-school activities, dinner, then getting everyone settled for the evening. It seemed to be working for the most part, and I felt we'd found a way to support each other and spend time together while still allowing everyone their own space.

"Did you have fun at Auntie Ellie's today?" I asked Catherine as she splashed water all over the bathroom floor.

"Ma." Catherine giggled as she hit water directly into my face.

"Thanks a lot." I laughed back and splashed some in her direction.

Of course, Catherine thought this was a game and hit me again, which earned her a splash in return. I loved these little games with my daughter, but by the time I'd had enough and put a stop to things, Catherine had managed to flood the entire bathroom. I picked her up, wrapped her in a large towel, and carried her into Zak and my bedroom. Zak had lit the gas fireplace earlier in the evening, so it was nice and toasty warm. I laid Catherine on the bed next to my cats, Marlow and Spade, while I went to the attached nursery to find her footie pajamas. Marlow, who was usually the more playful of the cats, wasn't a fan of having his fur pulled, but surprisingly, Spade, who has always been the quieter of the two, seemed to love the whole baby package.

"Da," Catherine screamed when Zak walked into the room with an arm full of folded laundry.

Zak set the pile on the dresser, then scooped her up and, cradling her in his arms, began to give her belly kisses, which made her laugh and scream.

"You know, it's not a good idea to get her all wound up before bed," I scolded, even though I couldn't help but smile. I loved the way Zak played with our daughter, and the way she adored playing with him.

"I'll rock her after we get her dressed." Zak laid Catherine back down on the bed and began pulling on her jammies. "Everyone is occupied this evening, so I thought we'd just settle in up here. I'd like to discuss what happened this afternoon."

"I told you what happened." To be honest, I didn't want to rehash the whole thing. I knew Zak would be curious, but I was having a hard time getting the image of the man with the fang marks out of my mind and hoped for a distraction rather than a retelling.

"You gave me a very brief explanation of what occurred, but I'd like to discuss it in more detail," Zak countered. "It sounds like we might have a real maniac on the loose."

I sighed and plopped down onto the sofa while Zak settled into the rocker with Catherine and her nighttime bottle. I wanted to forget about the man I'd found that afternoon, though I did find myself speculating about him. Salinger hadn't called, so I guessed he didn't have an ID yet, but still I wondered. Was he someone's father? Husband? Brother or son? Had he died as part of a game aimed at me, or had the motive for murder had to do with him, with me as a side plot? I supposed it was possible he'd been killed by a jealous wife, a vengeful neighbor, or a wronged employee, but that wouldn't explain the puncture wounds that looked like a vampire bite or that he'd been found in the most haunted place on the mountain.

I pulled a throw over my lap and snuggled up with one of the pillows we'd arranged on both ends of the seating area. When I was snuggly and content I began to speak. "Do you remember when the ghost hunter died in that house four years ago?"

Zak cradled Catherine close to his chest and began to sway back and forth as he lulled her toward sleep. "I remember. His name was Adam Davenport and he came to study paranormal activity in the house. I also remember I almost lost you to the madman who killed him."

"I know. I remember as well, although, looking back, I'm not sure Joel Ringer ever meant to kill me. I'm pretty sure his only intention was to detain me. Debating that issue isn't the reason I brought it up, however. Do you remember that huge storm we got caught in that same Halloween, when we found Karloff on the side of the road? We'd been heading out to the Henderson House to investigate when Karloff ran out in front of us and you just barely missed hitting him."

"Yes. But what's that about? We didn't hit him, and he found a good home with Levi, so everything worked out in the end."

"Everything did work out in the end. In fact, it was that Halloween when we finally got engaged. But that isn't my point either. At least not totally."

"Okay. So what's your point?"

I leaned toward Zak slightly. "After we found the pup we brought him home and got him settled. Do you remember what we did after that?"

Zak furrowed his brow; then he must have remembered because he grinned. "I do remember what we did after that."

"I miss that." I glanced at Catherine, as I once again let the memory play through my mind. We'd come home, built a fire, settled the puppy, then retired to our indoor/outdoor spa with a bottle of champagne. After that we'd come upstairs and spent the night in each other's arms. "Don't get me wrong. I love our family. I love having a house filled with love, several generations, and more activities than we can reasonably manage. But sometimes, when I think back to those days, like I did as I was driving through the storm to the house today, I realize that while I love what we have, at times I miss what we had."

Zak sent me a tender look. "I guess it's hard to have a romantic night outdoors in the spa with a house full of people, but once Catherine goes to bed we'll have this suite to ourselves."

"We will," I agreed. "And I look forward to that. But I guess I'm in one of my melancholy moods. I have been for a while, and I don't know why. It doesn't make any sense, really. I have everything to be happy about, but sometimes I can't help but feel sad."

Zak stood up with our sleeping baby in his arms. "It does make sense. And I sometimes feel the same way. In the past four years we've had a baby, accepted guardianship of two teenagers, and invited another adult, who requires her own level of supervision, into our home. It's a lot, and while I love every minute of the life we've built, I do sometimes miss *us* as well." Zak walked into the nursery and put Catherine down in her crib. Then he came back into the bedroom. He took my hand and led me to the French doors leading out onto the deck that was exclusive to this suite. It had stopped raining, and the clouds had cleared, revealing the stars and moon shining down on the still water of the lake. "You know," he said, pulling me closer to his side, "it wouldn't take much effort to add a hot tub out here." He pointed to a dark corner. "Maybe over there. Near the railing."

I tightened the fingers of the hand Zak was holding. "A hot tub for two?"

"Absolutely a hot tub for two. A no-kids-or-grandmothers-allowed hot tub for two."

I leaned my head against Zak's shoulder and looked out over the clear dark night. "That sounds absolutely perfect."

Chapter 3

Tuesday, October 23

Zak and I never had gotten around to discussing the vampire murder the previous evening. He'd brought it up, but then we began to discuss the hot tub, and one thing led to another, and, well, you know. Talk of death and haunted houses pretty much was forgotten. He'd had an early meeting at Zimmerman Academy this morning, so we hadn't talked then either, but I was under no illusions that he'd forget about it or let it go.

I got everyone off to school, then decided to head into town to pick up a Halloween costume for Catherine, as well as some candy and party favors for the children who would be attending our party. As I expected, the Halloween store was crowded, but Catherine loved the people and I loved the decorations, so we were both happy as we wandered the aisles. I'd invited Nona to come with us, but she'd claimed she had a headache and opted to skip it.

"So, what do you think?" I asked Catherine as I held up a selection of outfits. "Cookie Monster? Minnie Mouse? Maybe Winnie the Pooh?"

Catherine seemed more interested in watching the baby seated in a stroller at the other end of the aisle than the costumes I held up, so it appeared it was up to me. Both the Cookie Monster and the Winnie the Pooh costumes were thick and fuzzy, which would be perfect for trick-or-treating if we decided to take her out. On the other hand, both would probably be too hot to wear indoors for any length of time. Minnie Mouse was cute, but I wasn't sure. I definitely didn't want to go the princess route. Maybe a doggy or kitty costume?

"Oh my, look at this." I held up a lamb costume that was one-piece but not quite as heavy as Cookie Monster or Winnie, fuzzy beige with big floppy black ears. It was adorable. "What do you think? Do you want to be a lamb?"

Catherine pointed at the baby in the stroller, who happened to be chewing on a toddler cookie.

"Yes, I see the other baby has a cookie. I don't have any with me, but I do have juice."

Catherine reached for the bottle I held up and I tossed the lamb costume into the basket. Now I needed toys and candy for the little gift bags I wanted to create for the kids. I was pretty sure I'd seen small items in the front of the store, so I headed in that direction. There, I found Zimmerman Academy principal Phyllis King sorting through a bin of rubber spiders.

"I like the one with the red eyes," I said, walking up behind her.

Phyllis turned. "Zoe, Catherine. How nice to see you both." Phyllis glanced in my basket. "It looks like someone's going to be an adorable little lamb for Halloween."

I held up the costume. "It's pretty cute, and it's warm without being too heavy. Are you buying decorations for the dance?"

"Zak already has that covered, but I wanted to decorate my office with a few pumpkins and spiders. I spoke to him this morning and he told me that you had a bit of excitement yesterday."

"If you can call finding the victim of a vampire attack exciting."

"Zak mentioned the puncture wounds, but surely you don't actually believe…"

"I don't," I interrupted. "At least I don't think I do. It was pretty creepy, though. Did Zak tell you that it looked like I was intentionally steered toward the house so I'd discover the victim?"

"He did. That worries me."

I bit my bottom lip. "It worries me as well, although I'm trying very hard to convince myself that I'm in absolutely no danger. I don't suppose you've heard anything?"

"About the murder or the person who carried it out, no. I might know something about the victim."

"Such as?"

Phyllis brushed a lock of her long white hair away from her face. "When Zak told me the man who was found in the basement didn't have any identification and didn't look familiar to either you or Salinger, I remembered a man I ran into at Rosie's Café a few days ago. He was talking to the cashier, who stopped me and introduced us. His name was Edgar Irvine, and he was a visitor to Ashton Falls. He needed directions to the old cemetery outside of town and said the cashier thought I might be able to help."

"Which cemetery?" I asked.

"The one near the foot of the mountain where we held our Halloween event a few years ago."

"The one where Isaac Wainwright is buried?" I confirmed, referring to the source of another local legend.

"Yes, that's the one. I gave him directions, though, knowing no one has been buried there in a century or more, I asked him why he was interested in it. He said he was writing a screenplay about a group of ghost hunters who visit haunted places. He didn't mention Henderson House specifically, but he said there were three places on his list to see. I would think if someone was researching haunted places, Henderson House would be one of them."

"I agree. What did he look like?"

"Tall. Dark hair. Skinny. I called Salinger and described him, and he said it sounded as if we might have a match, so he sent me a photo." Phyllis made an unpleasant face. "It was an after photo, I'm afraid, but the man who asked for directions was definitely the victim."

This was an unexpected twist. The man I'd found in the most haunted house in town had been asking for directions to the most haunted cemetery in the area. "Out of all the haunted places in this county alone, I wonder why he decided to investigate haunted places in Ashton Falls. We're just a tiny little town most people have never even heard of."

"I don't know," Phyllis admitted. "He didn't say why he chose Ashton Falls. I guess you can ask Sheriff Salinger if he was able to ascertain the man's reason for being here in the first place. He told me that he planned to go to the man's hotel room to see what he could find there: notes, a computer, something that might provide a lead to what he was after and who might have wanted him dead."

"The day you ran into him at Rosie's, when you gave him directions, did it seem as if he planned to head out to the cemetery right away?"

"I think so. Which would mean if he had three places on his list, it's likely Henderson House was his last stop. Again, Salinger might be able to answer your questions about him by this point."

Asking Salinger about Edgar Irvine was exactly what I was going to do. But first I needed to meet Ellie for lunch to find out if I was going to have an honorary niece or nephew.

******

"So?" I asked her, after I'd placed Catherine in a high chair and slid into the booth where she was already waiting with Eli.

Ellie smiled. "We're having a girl."

I clasped my hands together. "A girl! I'm so happy for you."

"I'm happy too. I honestly didn't know if I wanted a boy or a girl when I went into the doctor's office, but when he said it was a girl I felt this extreme joy in my heart. I seriously felt like jumping off the table and hugging him."

I reached across the table, grabbed Ellie's hands, and gave them a squeeze. "I'm so excited. Catherine is excited too." I looked at Catherine, who appeared to be more interested in the cracker I had given her than our conversation. "How does Levi feel about having a girl?"

"He seems to be really happy." Ellie paused. "I wasn't sure he would be. He talks about sons all the time, not really about daughters. He's always saying he's going to teach his sons to play football and baseball, and how he can't wait until Eli is old enough to go hiking or fishing. He even talks about having sons to carry on his family name, but he's never talked about wanting a daughter, so I wasn't sure what to expect, but when the doctor gave us the news he seemed happy. I hope he's happy."

"I'm sure he is. Zak adores having a little princess to dote on. I'm sure Levi will as well. In fact, I'm fairly certain he's going to spoil her rotten. Do you have a name picked out?"

Ellie shook her head. "No. We've discussed and discarded a lot of them, but I don't feel we've hit on the right one. We have two months to decide. I'm sure we can figure it out now that we know for certain we're having a girl."

"We need to go shopping," I said. "If you're having a girl you won't be able to use Eli's hand-me-downs like you said at one point. I know I didn't want a lot of pink, frilly stuff for Catherine, but pink and frilly seems like a must for a Denton daughter. Maybe we can go to the mall in Bryton Lake before the Christmas rush sets in. I think we have a few more weeks at least before the crowds become unmanageable."

"I think we have time," Ellie agreed. "It's not even Halloween, although the Christmas hoopla seems to get started earlier every year. Did you find a costume for Catherine?"

I filled Ellie in on everything I'd purchased that morning. When I got to the part about running into Phyllis, I shared the most recent update on Ashton Fall's newest murder as well.

"Wow, that's really strange," Ellie said. "Four years ago a ghost hunter died in the Henderson House, and now a man writing a screenplay about haunted places ends up dead in the same house. What are the odds?"

"Probably pretty low if everything happened by chance. But what if that isn't how it happened?"

"I know you think the murder scene was set up as part of a sick game to involve you, but does it also mean you think Edgar Irvine was intentionally lured here?"

"I suppose it would be pretty far out of the realm of reality to think anyone would go to that much trouble to stage the perfect murder scene, but the thought has occurred to me. The fact that the man was here to investigate haunted places might simply have put him at the scene at the time the killer needed a victim."

Ellie's smiled faded. "If this guy was lured here, I'm terrified for you. Talk about premeditation. It almost seems like the killer could have been working on this for weeks, or even months."

I took in a breath and then blew it out. "Yeah. It's beginning to feel like something out of a horror movie." I tried to squash down the feeling of dread in my chest.

"Maybe you should take the kids and go on a trip. Go visit your relatives in Switzerland. It seems like a needless risk to stay here if you're the object of someone's obsession."

"I can't just run off to Switzerland."

"Sure you can. Your husband has access to a private jet and a bazillion dollars. He could take you away from Ashton Falls and the danger that appears to be lurking about in a flash."

"Okay, then I *won't* just run off to Switzerland. We don't even know for certain I'm in any real danger. Sure, there are circumstances that indicate there's someone out there playing with me, but it's also possible we could be reading things wrong."

Ellie gave me a firm look. "I know you want to face this the way you face everything else: head-on. But I'm really worried. If you won't go out of town will you at least stay home?"

I hesitated. "I understand the danger, if there's some madman fixated on me. I do. And while I don't plan to jump feet first into any type of investigation, I don't feel like staying totally out of the loop; not being aware of what's going on isn't a good choice either." I glanced at Catherine. "I'd like to stop by to see what Salinger's found out. Would you mind taking Catherine home with you? I'll come to get her as soon as I get the update."

Ellie sighed, but I could see she'd reconciled herself to my decision. "I'm happy to take Catherine home with me. She and Eli are due for naps anyway. But promise me you'll be careful."

"I will. My plan is to talk to Salinger. Nothing more."

Ellie rolled her eyes. "I can't tell you how many times I've heard that. You do realize the number of times you've found yourself close to death greatly exceeds the national average."

"I know."

"By a lot," Ellie emphasized.

"I know. But I'll be careful this time. I promise. I know it seems logical that I should want to hide out where no one can find me, but I need to know what to expect so I can be prepared. What if this horrific game isn't over? What if the vampire comes after someone I love if they can't get to me?"

Ellie frowned. "You think they would?"

I shrugged. "I don't know, but I don't want to risk it. I know you're worried, but I promise I'll come over to the boathouse right after I stop at the sheriff's office so you can see that I'm safe and sound."

Ellie blew out a slow breath. "Okay. I suppose you're going to do what you're going to do anyway. It does provide me with a small amount of comfort that Catherine will be safe with me while her mommy plays Nancy Drew."

Chapter 4

Salinger was just finishing up a phone call when I arrived at his office. He motioned for me to take a seat. His desk was piled higher with paperwork and folders than usual. It looked like he'd been busy, which was good, because maybe that meant he had something.

As soon as he hung up, he tossed a popular tabloid across the desk. I picked it up and looked at the front page. The headline read: `Man dies from vampire attack in Ashton Falls.`

"How is this even possible?" I asked. "It's been less than twenty-four hours since the body was found. This article had to have been printed yesterday for it to have reached the newsstands this morning."

"I've been asking myself that question since the article was pointed out to me. The only thing I can come up with is that the killer submitted the article himself before you even found the body."

"Do you think someone from the paper can tell us who submitted the article?" I asked.

"I was speaking to the editor when you came in. The piece was delivered anonymously. He said they don't do a lot to verify the tips they receive because the whole point of their publication is to publish shocking headlines to sell papers."

I picked it up again. "This is bad."

Salinger nodded. "If I had to guess, the town is going to be overflowing with wackos wanting to see a real vampire before the sun sets on another day."

I looked across the desk at Salinger. "Do you think the person behind this is after the hoopla it will bring all along?"

Salinger shrugged. "Maybe."

"So what do we do?"

"Solve the murder, run a feature with the actual facts in a reputable newspaper, and try to quell the vampire hype."

"We need to solve this case and solve it fast. I ran into Phyllis. She said she provided you with information about where the victim was staying. Did you find something that will help us figure this out?"

Salinger sat back in his chair. "Something, yes, but unfortunately, not as much as we need."

I leaned forward, resting my arms on the desk in front of me. "Okay. What do you know?"

He hesitated.

"Come on, Salinger. I know you don't want me involved, but I am. Being kept in the dark isn't going to help me. It'll be better if I know what's going on so I can keep an eye out for anything that seems relevant to the situation. Besides, maybe I can help. We both want this wrapped up sooner rather than later."

"Okay. I guess you have a point." He picked up a folder and began to tell me what he found inside.

"Our victim is a man named Edgar Irvine. He lives in Hollywood, California, where he works as a writer focusing on paranormal activity. It appears he was fairly successful as a screenwriter who'd sold many scripts and published several books. From the e-mails we found on his computer, it appears he was sent information about three sites in Ashton Falls that are rumored to have a history of paranormal activity: Henderson House, the cemetery where Isaac Wainwright is buried, and the old Norlander mine."

I remembered that Alex was researching the Norlander mine for her school paper and hoped showing interest in it wouldn't put her in any danger. Maybe I'd suggest she choose a different topic.

"It seems," Salinger continued, "that Irvine was sent enough information to capture his interest. He arrived in Ashton Falls on Friday."

"Where was he staying?"

"The inn. As far as I can tell, he checked in at about four thirty that afternoon. He was seen leaving the inn on foot at around seven. He'd mentioned to a desk clerk that he planned to grab a bite to eat. The clerk said he returned at around nine. The morning clerk didn't see him leave the next day, but his room was empty when housekeeping went in to tidy up at around ten. He didn't know what Irvine's plans were for the day on Saturday, but Phyllis saw him at Rosie's, when he asked for directions to the cemetery. We're assuming that's where he went. A clerk saw him come back to the inn at around five." Salinger took a breath before he continued. "No one saw Irvine either leave or return to the inn on Sunday, but he wasn't in his room when housekeeping showed up at around eleven thirty to clean the room, and he was seen leaving the inn on Monday morning at around nine, so we know he returned at some point. You found his body at Henderson House at around five o'clock on Monday. The coroner put time of death at around three o'clock. We don't know where he was between nine and three."

Wow. Salinger *had* been busy. I took a minute to review the details, then asked the question at the forefront of my mind. "So this man was in town in response to information he'd been sent. Do we know who sent it to him?"

"The e-mails were signed by Boris Grimly. There's no personal information in them. I have the tech guys looking into things, but so far we haven't been able to trace them back to a server."

"So there's no way to know who sent it."

"Not yet."

"Are we thinking this Grimly lured Irvine to town and then killed him?"

"Perhaps."

"Why go to all that trouble, and why involve me?"

Salinger shook his head. "At this point we don't know that Grimly killed Irvine, or that he intentionally involved you. All we really know is that a writer came to town to investigate haunted places near Ashton Falls and ended up dead inside one of them."

I sat back and groaned. This was getting frustrating. "If Irvine got into town on Friday and was killed on Monday, it's likely he came into contact with other people in town. He might even have hired a car or made calls for information. I don't suppose you found Irvine's phone?"

Salinger shook his head. "No phone. I've requested his phone records. And I have a call in to both his agent and his publisher. I figured one or both might know more about the person who sent him the information. Now that we have the victim's name we should be able to put together a profile."

I tucked a sneakered foot under my leg, adjusting my position slightly. "Okay, so we know who the victim is, and we know when and where he died. Do we know *how* he died?"

"Snake venom."

I raised a brow. "Snake venom?"

"The two puncture wounds on his neck weren't left by a vampire but by some device that injected the venom into his bloodstream."

I frowned. "A device was used? He wasn't actually bitten by a snake?"

"The coroner has determined that, while he died as a result of snake venom in his bloodstream, the method of delivery was something artificial. He isn't sure what was used, but he's working on it."

"What type of venom?" I asked.

"The lab is trying to figure that out as well. The venom had to have been from an extremely lethal variety of snake because death came very quickly."

"So someone either purchased venom or had a snake with them from which they harvested the venom, then used it to kill Irvine to make it appear as if he'd been bitten by a vampire. Then they contacted a popular tabloid to leak the story that there was a vampire loose in Ashton Falls. Again, I have to ask why."

"We don't know for certain that the killer was the one who leaked the story, although given the timing, it seems likely. As for the rest, it's early in the investigation and we don't have all the details, so all we have so far is speculation. The house was searched and no snake of any kind was found, so I'm thinking the killer either never had the snake there or they took the snake with them when they left."

I couldn't help but shudder. I certainly hoped there hadn't been a snake in the room with me when I was at the house. I won't say I hate snakes and want the world rid of them, but I've never been able to warm up to them either. "Where does this leave us at this point?"

"It doesn't leave *us* anywhere," Salinger answered. "I'm doing research and you're staying out of it. Remember?"

I huffed out a breath. "Yes, I remember."

"Go home, play with your baby, and let me track down Edgar Irvine's killer. Once I have answers to all these questions I'll fill you in."

"But—"

"No buts. I promised that very supportive husband of yours that I'd keep you away from any danger that might come looking for you, and that's exactly what I intend to do. Now go home."

"Oh, all right," I grumbled. "But if you find out anything call me. This not-knowing stuff isn't working for me at all."

******

When I arrived at Ellie's, both babies were still fast asleep, so I settled in with a cup of tea for a nice long visit. Ellie and I used to hang out all the time, but since we'd both become mothers, our sitting-and-chatting time had been reduced greatly. After I'd assured Ellie that Salinger had everything under control, she wanted to discuss baby names, nursery themes, and bedding colors, and I was happy to oblige. To a degree.

"Are you even listening to me?" Ellie said at some point in the conversation.

"Sure. You were talking about candy."

"I was talking about paint."

I furrowed my brow. "No. I specifically remember you saying something about cotton candy and candy apples."

"Cotton-candy pink and candy-apple red are paint shades. It's okay if you want to talk about something else."

I let out a sigh. "I'm sorry. I know you're excited about decorating the nursery, and I know I said Salinger had everything under control, but I can't get the man in the basement out of my mind."

Ellie frowned. "There's more to this, isn't there? Something you aren't telling me."

"There've been a few developments," I admitted.

"So share."

"For one thing, Salinger told me snake venom was delivered to Irvine's bloodstream via some sort of a device that mimicked a vampire's bite. I thought the vampire thing was a ploy to somehow get at me because it seemed I was being maneuvered into finding the body, but Salinger also said he was sent a tip that a popular tabloid published an article about a vampire attack in Ashton Falls."

"Already? How's that even possible?"

"I don't know. He thinks the killer may have sent in the information in the article even before I found

49

the body. He talked to the tabloid people, and they said they got the tip anonymously."

"This is bad," Ellie said. "The town is going to be overrun with vampire hunters."

"That's what Salinger and I think as well. He's working on trying to come up with some real answers to counteract the hype. He knows who the victim is now, and that will help him to gather additional information. In the meantime, I think we should prepare for the worst. Salinger keeps telling me to let him handle it, to try not to think about it, but trying not to think about it is making me think about it constantly. I'm going to go crazy if it goes on too long."

"Then let's talk about something else. I can see you didn't find my exposition on paint colors riveting, but earlier, you mentioned we should discuss food for the Halloween party. With all the baby talk, we never got around to it at lunch."

"And you have some ideas?"

"Of course." Ellie jumped up. "Hang on. I'll grab my list."

I checked my phone while I waited for her to come back from the kitchen. There was a text from Jeremy, letting me know someone had been in the Zoo looking for me. He hadn't left a message, but he'd said his name was Orson Spalding, and he'd given Jeremy his e-mail address to forward to me. Jeremy thought he remembered seeing Orson somewhere before, although he couldn't remember where, maybe our last adoption clinic.

I texted Jeremy back to say I'd get in touch with Orson. If he had questions about adopting a pet, Jeremy was well qualified to answer them, but there were still a lot of people who insisted on speaking to the shelter owner. I supposed I understood that. If something was really important to me, I wanted to speak to the owner of a business too.

"Something up?" Ellie asked when she returned with the list.

"Just a message from Jeremy about a guy who wants me to e-mail him. Just give me a sec and I'll respond to him, then I'm all yours." I used my phone to send the e-mail. Then I put my phone in my pocket and turned my attention to Ellie. "So, bat-shaped wontons?"

"Among other things, including stuffed intestines, jack-o'-lantern pizzas, and rat cakes."

I made a face. "Rat cakes?"

"They're just little cakes made to look like rats. No actual rats will be used in the production of the cakes. I'm going to cut up some fruit in fun shapes for the younger kids. We aren't going to want them to get all sugared up."

"I saw this thing on the internet where someone made meatloaf shaped like a face. A very messed-up face. It was called a zombie loaf. I seem to remember they used little onions as eyes and small crackers as teeth."

"I'm not sure I'd want to eat something shaped like a face. Besides, I was thinking we'd stick to finger foods. Which reminds me: we'll need mummy fingers."

By the time the babies woke up from their naps, Ellie and I had settled on the menu. Zak and Ellie would handle most of the cooking, but it was nice to be included in the process. Ellie's enthusiasm had gone a long way toward helping me to look forward to the party. It was going to be a busy few days, with Haunted Hamlet this weekend, followed by the Halloween party on Wednesday of next week, but after a few hours with my energetic friend I felt up for it.

Chapter 5

Wednesday, October 24

As predicted, by the following day the vampire hype had become a living, breathing thing as vampire hunters from all over the country congregated in Ashton Falls to celebrate the undead in the hope of meeting the creature who'd killed Edgar Irvine in the flesh.

"This is crazy," Tawny Upton, a fellow events committee member, complained during our last meeting before Haunted Hamlet, which was set to run Friday through Sunday. "The town is so full of vampire hunters and worshippers, there's nowhere for the visitors who want to come up for a family day at the festival to stay or even park. This vampire thing is going to ruin Haunted Hamlet."

"I don't disagree," I said. "I'm just not sure what we can do about it. The tabloid that first ran the story is all over it. There was a follow-up this morning. I spoke to Salinger about running an article offering proof that the bite marks were made by a device, not actual fangs, but he's dealing with an ongoing investigation and doesn't want to give too much away." I frowned. "In fact, I probably shouldn't even have mentioned it just now. I know you'll all be discreet."

Everyone promised they would. The committee, which usually had ten members, was a few short today. Normally, both Levi and Ellie attended, but Levi had an out-of-town football game and Ellie hadn't been feeling all that well when she woke up, so they were both out. Zak was tied up at the Academy and our newest member, Olivia Bradford, was away too, which left me, committee chairperson Hillary Spain, my new stepgrandmother, Hazel, preschool owner Tawny, my father, Hank Donovan, and novelty shop owner Gilda Reynolds.

"As it is, we've encountered more than our share of challenges with this year's event," Hillary said. "I can't emphasize enough how much the community needs the income our annual fund-raisers provide. I'm afraid with all the vampire enthusiasts around, the visitors we normally count on to come up from the valley simply won't."

"Maybe Salinger will figure this out soon and we can run something in the Bryton Lake newspaper at least," Hazel said encouragingly.

"Things are really out of our hands," my dad added. "I think all we can do is proceed as planned and hope everything works out."

"Have any of the food vendors made any noise about backing out?" Gilda asked.

"Not so far," Hillary said. "I wish I could say the vampire hunters will pick up the slack and spend the money in the local economy that will be lost if the families from the valley don't make the trip, but my impression of them is that they don't have a lot of money to spend. Most of them are camping out on the beach and in the park. There are signs discouraging such things, of course, but they're ignoring them. The hype will die down when they realize there are no vampires here. The question is whether that will happen in time."

We continued to discuss the situation for a while longer, but because there wasn't an answer to be had, Hillary called the meeting to an end.

After, I ran a few errands because my mom was watching Catherine. Originally, before I realized Ellie wasn't going to make it into town, the two of us had planned to grab some lunch, so my mom was already geared up to watch Catherine until at least one. I didn't have a lot of items to pick up for the party next week, though I wanted to avoid the last-minute rushing around that so often dominated my life. Now that I had a couple of hours to kill, I figured I may as well take care of the short list I'd created over the past few days.

My first stop was the Halloween store. Zak had the decorations for the house covered and then some, but I wanted to pick up some cute paper plates and napkins. The aisles that had once been stocked to overflowing were now showing bare spots as the holiday grew closer. I just hoped they'd have something cute left that didn't feature superheroes.

"*The Nightmare Before Christmas* napkins are pretty cute," my friend Erica said as I sorted through the items left on the shelf.

I smiled. "I did see those, and they are cute. Are you off today?" I asked. Erica usually worked at a local bar and grill.

"I work the late shift tonight. Worked the late shift last night too. I don't usually mind the late shift because the tips are better, but with the undead seekers in town, things have become pretty strange."

I picked up several packages of napkins and tossed them in my basket. "Yeah. Most of the locals aren't happy."

"I'm an open-minded person for the most part," Erica said, "but some of these people are really weird. Not all of them, of course. I've had decent conversations with several really nice people, but there are others..." Erica shivered. "This one guy came in last night and he had real fangs. Not removable; actual implants."

I grimaced. "Really? Who would do such a thing?"

"I don't know, but they were really creepy. He calls himself Lorcan. Then this other guy dressed all in black came in and threatened to put a stake through Lorcan's heart if he didn't clear out. Apparently, the second guy is some sort of vampire hunter." Erica leaned in just a bit. "I felt as if I was trapped in a really cheesy horror movie."

"Did you feel the second guy presented a real danger to the first one?" I asked.

Erica shrugged. "I don't think so. I mean, I kind of doubt the guy goes around staking people. I'm sure it's just part of some role-playing game. Still, Ashton

Falls isn't the sort of town where these things are normally played out. I wish they'd all just move on."

I really did intend to go directly to my mother's to pick up Catherine as soon as I finished my errands, but somehow I found myself driving to Henderson House. The fact that a psycho had not only killed a man but was threatening to disrupt a very important fund-raiser really stuck in my craw. Salinger couldn't make a statement about what was really going on until he closed the case, so the answer, it seemed, was to help him close it quickly.

I sat in my car for a minute after I pulled up outside the house. It looked the same as it always did, although minus the storm, it didn't seem quite as ominous as it had on Monday. I put my hand on the door latch, ignoring the voice in my head that was desperately trying to remind me that I'd promised both Zak and Salinger I was done with sleuthing. It wasn't that I wanted to break my promise. It was just that it was easier to promise not to get involved than it was to actually not get involved.

I carefully made my way up the stairs to the front door and stepped around the crime scene tape. I wasn't sure why the house had been left open all these years. It would have made sense to board the door closed, or at least fix the lock. There might have been fewer murders in Henderson House if someone had taken the time.

I'd just search the floors above the basement before heading down to the room where I'd found the body. I knew Salinger and his men had gone over the basement with a fine-tooth comb, but I wondered if they'd taken as much care with the attic and the two stories of living space.

Deciding to start at the top and work my way down, I headed up the rickety old stairs to the attic. Actually, I corrected myself as I made my way to the top of the staircase, the first place I was going to look was the secret crawl space from which props had been manipulated to scare the camp counselors who'd died in the house because of the madman who'd simply wanted to record their fear for a horror movie.

Despite my resolve to explore that space, my heart beat just a bit faster as I approached the hidden door. The last time I'd ventured into it I'd thought I was going to die. It wasn't a memory I wanted to relive.

The crawl space was cramped and windowless. Dust had settled over every surface, but otherwise it didn't appear as if the area had been disturbed since the day Zak rescued me there four years ago. Once my curiosity was assuaged, I headed to the attic. The large room had been empty when I'd been here last, but today I found an old mattress on the floor. I walked over to look out the window. With the exception of the old barn just behind the house, all I could see was trees for miles.

Then I searched the second floor, followed by the first, and eventually the basement. There wasn't anything to find, which wasn't surprising; Salinger's men would have been through everything. When I was certain the house held no clues, I went outside. As I approached my vehicle, I remembered the barn. I turned away from the car and headed down the drive and around the house. I realized there was little chance I'd find anything there, but it seemed worth looking, if only to reassure myself that I'd been thorough.

Like the house, the barn was dark and dusty. There was a hay loft overhead and half-rotted stalls below. The old stairs leading up to the loft looked even more rickety than the stairs in the house and I was about to leave when an instinct, or maybe it was my Zodar, urged me to go up.

The old stairs were really no more than a rotted wooden ladder. I tested my weight on the first rung. It held, so I used my arms on the rungs in front of my body to pull myself up to the second rung. The fourth and sixth rungs gave way under my feet, but eventually, I was able to make it up to the loft without slipping down. I paused and looked around. From the boxes stacked along the back wall, it appeared someone had used the barn for storage at some time. From a glance, I didn't notice anything that would qualify as a clue to who had killed Edgar Irvine, but I was curious about the boxes, so I crossed the loft to lift the lid of the first one.

I gasped, and my heart began to race even faster as I took out my phone to call Salinger.

******

I watched as he sorted through the contents of the first box, a look of increasing horror on his face. Horror was exactly what I'd been feeling when I'd opened that box and realized what was inside.

"What do you think?" I asked.

Salinger held up a photo of me standing in front of Zoe's Zoo talking to Jeremy. I was holding Catherine, and Charlie was standing next to me. "It looks like you have a stalker."

"That's what I thought when I realized the box was full of photos of me. Some were taken outside my house, while others were taken while I was at work or in town. And they look fairly recent."

Salinger scowled as he studied the photo in his hand. "How recent?"

"The one you're holding was taken on Friday of last week. I was out doing errands with Catherine and Charlie and stopped by the Zoo to ask Jeremy about a mountain lion cub that was supposed to be brought in." I walked across the loft and took the photo from Salinger. "This looks like it was taken with one of those old Polaroids." I glanced up at Salinger. "Do they even make those anymore?"

"They do, but with a more modern design and a better quality. This photo might have been taken on a pretty old version, but I don't know where someone would get film for it." There was an expression of outrage on Salinger's face.

"Who do you think took these?"

He angrily tossed the photo into the box and mumbled a series of curses before he spoke directly to me. "I don't know."

"Do you think the photos are connected to Irvine's body, or that the entire town seems to have been invaded by vampire hunters? Do you think whoever's been stalking me also killed Edgar Irvine?"

"I don't know that either. What I do know is that heads are going to roll when I confront the men I told to search this property. They should have found these."

I glanced around the dark and dusty barn. I wasn't sure when it had last been used for its original purpose, but I was pretty sure it hadn't been during my lifetime. "I suppose they must have focused on the basement because that's where the body was found," I offered. "The only way to know the boxes were up here would be to climb up, and the ladder is in pretty bad condition."

"That's no excuse. You found the photos and it wasn't even your job to look for them." Salinger frowned. "Why were you up here anyway? I thought you were going to stay out of this."

"I was, but things in town are really tense with all the vampire hunters, so I decided to take a look around here. I know I shouldn't have, but I'm glad I did."

Salinger didn't answer, but I could see he was furious. I wasn't sure if he was angry with me or his men or both, but I felt it best to change the subject.

"I heard there are people in town who have real fangs; not the kind you can pop in and out but permanent implants."

Salinger lifted a brow. "Really? Who would want to have those?"

"I'm not sure, but I met someone who told me that one of these vampire wannabes with real fangs ran into a guy who claimed to be a vampire hunter in the bar where she works last night. The hunter threatened to stake the guy with the fangs if he didn't move on. I know this is over-the-top ridiculous, but I found myself wondering if we weren't going to find people around town who'd been staked to death."

Salinger kicked at a bale of old hay. "This has gotten completely out of control. One way or another, I'm running these particular visitors out of town."

"It won't be easy."

Salinger grunted as he knelt down and started sorting through the photos in another box. It seemed like a good time to move on. "I need to go pick up Catherine. If you have any questions for me feel free to call."

Chapter 6

Later that evening, after the kids had gone up to their rooms to do homework and Nona had retired to her suite to watch television, I decided to come clean with Zak about the photographs. I really, really didn't want him to freak out, but I realized I could be in real danger, and I didn't want to keep something so important from him.

"Can we talk?" I asked after we'd settled Catherine in her crib.

Zak took my hand and led me to the sofa. "Okay. What do you want to talk about?"

"I told you it seemed someone might have staged the death of Edgar Irvine, the writer, to mimic Coach Griswold's death. We also discussed the fact that his death was made to look like a vampire attack. What you don't know is that I found something else in the Henderson barn today. Something even more disturbing."

"What did you find?"

"A box of photos. Photos of me. All taken within the last month. Maybe even the past couple of weeks."

Zak sucked in a breath. "Someone's been following you and taking photos?"

I nodded. "It would appear so. I have a stalker, but I don't know if he means me harm. I thought you should know."

Zak pursed his lips and narrowed his gaze. "I don't like this one bit. I'm hiring a bodyguard to be with you when I can't be."

I shook my head. "No bodyguard. We don't know if my stalker is dangerous."

"A man is dead."

I let out a slow breath. "Well, yeah. There is that."

"Were any of the photos taken here at the house?"

"A few. Not inside, but there are some of me walking on the beach."

"Were there any of anyone other than you?" Zak asked. "The kids?"

I cringed. "There were a few photos of me with Catherine."

Zak stood up. "Okay, it's settled. We're keeping the kids home from school until this is taken care of. You," Zak looked at me with an expression that left no room for argument, "are staying here as well."

"Wait." I shot out a hand and stood up myself. "I won't be held prisoner in my own home."

Zak's face grew red. He looked mad, but I supposed he might just be scared. "So you'd rather risk your life and the life of the children?"

"No," I insisted. "I'd never intentionally put the kids in danger. But maybe we can come to a compromise."

Zak took a deep breath but didn't speak.

"Please," I added, "I don't want to put myself or the kids in danger, but I need to find out who this stalker is or I'll never be able to feel safe. Maybe we can work together on this. Like the old days."

Zak's expression softened a bit. "I'm listening."

I paused before I continued. This conversation could easily get out of hand if we let it. "How about if we keep the kids home from school for the time being and I agree to only leave the grounds if I'm with you or Salinger?"

Zak sat back. I was glad he was at least considering my suggestion. "I'd prefer you stay here all the time, but I know you probably won't, and I'd feel better if you were with me or Salinger. But Catherine, Alex, and Scooter don't leave the house. Nona either for that matter. If this stalker already has been following you for weeks, chances are he knows who you're close to. If he's the one who killed the man you found in the Henderson basement, he's dangerous. If he can't get to you directly he might be satisfied with getting to you through them."

"Okay. I'll talk to the kids."

Zak stood up and took my hand in his. "Now that we have that settled, let's go downstairs to the computers to see if we can find something that will help us nail this wacko."

When we arrived in the computer room Zak called Phyllis to let her know that both he and Alex would be taking a few days off from Zimmerman Academy. We'd need to call Scooter's school tomorrow. Then Zak logged onto the computer and typed in some commands. "Do you think your stalker is someone from your past?" he asked.

I shrugged. "I can't think of a single person who would follow me around taking photos of me. And I can't see how I'm in any way related to or associated with Edgar Irvine. Why would my stalker kill him? If my stalker didn't kill him, do we have two bad guys to worry about?"

"Let me see what I can dig up on Irvine."

I sat down in a chair next to him.

After a few minutes Zak said, "It looks as if the e-mail Irvine received from this Boris Grimly came from a cell phone. A burner cell, naturally, but I can see the e-mail came from right here in Ashton Falls. Apparently, it looks as if Irvine received six e-mails from the same phone over a two-month period."

"Two months? That means his killer has been working on this plot for a while."

"So it would seem."

"So why Irvine, and why Ashton Falls? He lived in Hollywood, so why did his killer go to the trouble of luring him here? Why not travel to LA and shoot him there? In a city with more homicides, one more shooting would hardly be noticed. At least not to the degree a vampire murder has been in Ashton Falls."

"I think that may be the point," Zak said. "The killer wanted the hype. Not only did he kill a man in a very strange manner, he made sure the tabloids would pick it up by tipping them off before it even happened."

"Seems the killer is setting himself up to get caught."

"Maybe. While he seems to be looking for attention, he's been careful to cover his tracks. The burner cell was paid for with cash, so it's untraceable, and he killed Irvine with a fang device without leaving behind any fingerprints or DNA. At least not any the crime scene people have found yet. His moves have been quite calculated."

"So why involve me?"

The crease in Zak's forehead deepened. He went back to typing and I continued to watch. It was clear he was in the zone, so I didn't want to distract him with any more questions or concerns. I enjoyed watching him work. Knowing he could hack into databases very few others could was kind of a turn-on.

"Irvine's passport indicates he's traveled widely. His last trip was about six months ago. Other than that, he seems to have lived fairly frugally. I'm not picking up any extravagant or irregular activity in his bank records." Zak paused and sat back in his chair. "There's a monthly payment of one thousand dollars to someone named Carl Poland."

"Doesn't that seem odd?" I asked.

"Not necessarily. It's possible Irvine purchased something from Poland and was making monthly payments. He might have borrowed money from Poland and was paying him back. Maybe Poland was a friend or relative who was down on his luck and Irvine was helping him out. There are a lot of legitimate reasons why someone would transfer a thousand dollars a month to another person." Zak drummed his fingers on the table in front of him. "Having said that, I think it would be worth our while to do some digging to see if we can find out exactly who Poland is and how he was related to Irvine." Zak jotted down a note. "I'm going to take a more in-depth look at Irvine's phone records as well. Salinger only pulled records from the past couple of weeks; I'd like to see who Irvine spoke to on a regular basis prior to coming to Ashton Falls." Zak looked at me. "Actually, that's something you can help me with."

I sat up a bit straighter. "It is?"

"I'm going to print out his phone records for the past six months. I want you to go through them and highlight any number that seems to appear more often than normal. I also want you to look for any unusual patterns that pop out. Like if there's a number he called every month on the first, and only on the first, highlight it. Or if there's a number that was called multiple times a day, highlight it."

Zak hit the Print command on the computer. Then he opened a drawer and took out a yellow highlighter. I went to work while he continued to dig in the nooks and crannies of Edgar Irvine's life. We worked silently side by side for about thirty minutes before Zak announced that Carl Poland was Irvine's assistant.

"So the money each month was payroll," I said.

"No, I don't think so," Zak said. "I found two sets of payments from Irvine to Poland. It looks like he started working for him two years ago. From what I can find, it looks like he's paid an hourly rate that's invoiced at the end of every month, which varies based on the number of hours he put in. The thousand dollars started about six months ago and is paid on the first of every month. The money paid to him as an assistant was being paid at the end of each month, so I'm thinking that's for something else."

"Something relevant to Irvine's death?"

"There's no way to know, but I'm thinking probably not."

"Was Poland Irvine's only assistant?" I wondered.

"No. It appears he had several. I suppose he might have hired different people for different sorts of tasks. It also looks like there was a high turnover, so he most likely used students or temp employees."

I stopped what I was doing and looked at Zak. "You know, these assistants—at least the more recent ones—might be able to provide us with some insight into what was going on in Irvine's life."

"Way ahead of you," Zak answered, picking up his cell. "Poland seems to have been Irvine's most recent assistant, and it appears he was with him for longer than any of the others I could find. I'll start with him and see where it leads."

While I waited for Zak to make his call, I called Ellie to fill her in on the photo situation. I didn't want to worry her, but if she found out before I had a chance to explain, she'd be hurt I hadn't confided in her. It also occurred to me that if the stalker had been following me for weeks he'd know who was closest to me, which theoretically could put those people in danger. Levi and Ellie were my closest friends; it seemed only right they should know to watch their backs. Maybe I'd even have Ellie and Eli come over here while Levi was at work. I didn't like the idea of them being home alone.

Ellie agreed she'd feel better spending the day with me while Levi was at school. None of us knew what was going on, but we realized it was best to take the situation seriously. I'd extended the same offer to Mom and Harper while my dad was at the store. Like Ellie, she agreed. Both planned to come by in the morning and spend the day.

Zak finished his call at the same time I did mine. "So?" I asked. "Did Poland know anything?"

"The information he shared was limited and guarded. I think he knew more than he was willing to discuss with me."

"What did he say?"

"Basically, that Irvine had several assistants at any one time. They all seemed to have their specialties and he used everyone to varying degrees. Poland said he was with Irvine for two years, longer than any other assistant by quite a bit. I asked what type of work he did for Irvine and he said mostly research. I asked if he'd helped with the research Irvine came to Ashton Falls to tackle and he said he hadn't. It seems the Ashton Falls trip came up all of a sudden, and as far as he knew, Irvine hadn't brought any of his usual assistants into the loop about it."

"Did he give you the names of the other assistants?"

"He mentioned two others. Both women. Both dealt only with piecework. He's going to e-mail their names and contact information. I'll follow up."

I stood up and walked around the room. This thing was definitely getting under my skin. There wasn't a single thing about Edgar Irvine that looped back to me in any way, shape, or form, so what was going on with the photos in the barn? Was it possible they really had nothing to do with Irvine, Grimly, or the vampire hunters who were taking over the town?

"So what now?" I asked. "I know you want me safe. I want me safe too. But there's no way I'm going to be able to just sit around and wait for whatever's going to happen."

Zak pulled me onto his lap. "I know this is hard for you. It is for both of us. But we've only been digging into this for a couple of hours. These things sometimes take time. All we can do is to keep going until we find what we're looking for. I'll call the other assistants as soon as I get their contact information, and I'll continue to dig around in bank, phone, employment, travel, and any other records I can find. We'll figure this out."

I laid my head on Zak's shoulder. "I'm just letting this get to me, I guess. I think I'll call Jeremy to let him know I won't be in tomorrow morning as I planned."

Zak went back to his research and I headed upstairs to make my call. I filled Jeremy in on what was happening and let him know I wouldn't be in until everything was resolved.

"I'm so sorry. I wish I could help. The only possible lead I have is on the stray you have at your house."

"That's great."

"It's not for sure, but I came across a lost-dog ad in the Bryton Lake newspaper from over a month ago. At first I thought it was unlikely our dog could have come from so far away, but then I realized if the killer intentionally picked it up, brought her to Henderson House, and tied her up in the basement, using a dog from out of the area was a good idea. Of course, that would mean the dog had either been a stray before that, or if it was with the killer, he would have been hanging on to her for a month, which also seemed unlikely."

"Yeah, I kind of doubt a killer would have taken care of the dog for a month. It's most likely another one, but let me know what you find out either way."

We chatted for a few more minutes before I hung up and went down the hall to check on the kids. I hated that the danger I was in was most likely going to mess up any plans they might have made for the weekend.

Chapter 7

Thursday, October 25

Zak went in to the Academy the next morning to pick up some papers he could work on at home, which meant Nona and I, and Mom and Ellie once they arrived, were alone with the kids. Zak and I hadn't had any breakthroughs the previous evening, but I was determined to maintain a positive attitude so as not to bring everyone else down with my negativity. Someone suggested baking cookies, so before I knew it, the house smelled of cinnamon and pumpkin.

"I used to love the pumpkin muffins you made when you had the restaurant," I said to Ellie. "The ones with the nuts and the cream cheese frosting."

"I can make you some when we're done with these. I'm pretty sure you have all the ingredients. If not, I can run over to my place."

"While I'd love to have some, I don't want you to go to that much trouble," I replied.

"I don't mind at all. I don't miss having to go into work every day, or the stress of trying to make the budget come out right at the end of the month, but I do miss having a reason to bake. I hardly ever do anymore. With so many people to eat everything, I may as well indulge."

Ellie indulging in baking meant I could indulge in eating, which seemed to me to work out just fine. As the others finished up the cookies, I went upstairs to call Jeremy. I'd forgotten to tell him about the woman who was bringing in a litter of kittens today. She'd called on Monday when he was off, and with everything going on, it had slipped my mind.

Afterward, I found myself lingering upstairs. The kitchen was filled with people I loved, but a few minutes of quiet felt like just what I needed. I hadn't been sleeping all that well this week, and the sleepless nights were beginning to get to me. Still, the crowd downstairs were having their lives disrupted because of me, so I really should head down.

I was about to join them when there was a knock on my door, and Alex poked her head in. "Can I come in?"

I waved her forward. "Do you feel like hiding too?"

Alex smiled. "No, it's not that. It's fun having Ellie and Grandma to bake with. I wish we could get together more often."

"Okay." I got up and moved from the desk to the sofa and patted a cushion next to me. "What's up?"

"It's the dance. I know we aren't supposed to leave home until everything's sorted out, but Diego and I have been really looking forward to it. Do you think this will be resolved by Saturday night?"

I put my arm around Alex and pulled her head to my shoulder. "I have no idea, but I want you and Scooter to be able to go to your dances. I'll talk to Zak about it. Both are being held in public places with a lot of chaperones. I'm sure it'll be fine."

Alex looked doubtful. "Zak was pretty upset when he talked to us earlier."

"He's scared, and he hasn't had a chance to really think things through." I tucked a lock of Alex's hair behind her ear. "Let me talk to him. We'll work something out. If nothing else, he can go to your dance as a chaperone. That way he can keep an eye on you while you hang out with your friends."

"What about Scooter?"

"If need be, Levi can go to his dance. And it's possible Zak and Sheriff Salinger will figure out who's been following me by Saturday anyway. They're both working hard on doing just that."

"Thanks, Zoe."

I sat up slightly and Alex did as well. "So, how is our mama doggy doing?" I asked.

"Really well. I think she's going to have the pups today. I set her up with a bed in the closet, and she's been in there since last night. I've been checking on her every hour or so. I think she'll have the first pup within the next couple of hours."

"I'm glad she has you to take care of her. I'm sure that gives her comfort."

"She's very sweet. I can't believe we still haven't found her owner. I thought for sure we would."

I bit my lower lip. "I wasn't going to mention it until I knew for sure, but Jeremy has a possible lead on a lost dog that fits the general description of this dog, although it's far from certain."

"Do you still think she was dognapped?"

I shrugged. "Jeremy found an ad in the newspaper in Bryton Lake, but it's a month old. It seems unlikely the killer would have hung on to the dog for a whole month. Still, it's worth looking in to."

"Bryton Lake." Alex tilted her head. "I figured she must be from around here."

"Maybe she started off as a stray, and whoever tied her up just happened to find her and got the idea to use her to lure me to the house."

"I hope you find her owner, but in the meantime she's doing fine with me. I'm enjoying her company and I'm excited to see the puppies. It's been a while since we've had babies in the house. Well, other than Catherine, that is." Alex paused. "Who I think I hear right now."

I stood up. "I'll get her. You go see to your mama. And tell Diego not to worry about the dance. One way or another, I'll make sure you're able to be there."

By the time I arrived in the nursery Catherine was standing up in her crib. When she saw me she began bouncing up and down while holding on to the top rail.

"Good morning, princess," I said as I opened my arms to her. "How was your nap?"

"Li-li."

"Yes, Eli's still here. I think he might be up from his nap too. Let's get you changed and we can go check."

"Da."

"Daddy's at work. He should be home soon, though." I lifted Catherine out of the crib and carried her to the changing table. "We have lots of people in the house for you to play with. Grandma's here. And Harper. You love Harper."

Catherine smiled. I wasn't sure whether she had any idea what I was talking about, but she seemed happy. Generally speaking, Catherine was a happy baby. If she was fussy there was usually a reason.

When she was changed we headed downstairs. I could hear the sound of laughter coming from the kitchen. There, I found Nona and my mom covered in flour.

"What on earth happened?" I asked.

"An experiment gone bad." Nona chuckled.

"Don't worry, we'll clean it up," Mom added.

Catherine reached for Harper as soon as she saw her, so I set her in her playpen, then lifted four-year-old Harper in with her. I didn't see either Eli or Ellie, so I figured he was either being fed or changed. I was sure he'd want to join the others in the playpen when he could.

"I think I'm going to take the dogs out, if someone can keep an eye on my little munchkin." I could see the argument in Mom's eyes, so I headed her off. "I'll stay on the grounds and I'll have eight dogs with me. I think I'll be perfectly safe."

"Okay," Mom said. "You're right. This thing just has me tense."

"Yeah, me too, but hopefully it will all be over soon, and we can resume our regularly scheduled lives."

It was a bright sunny day, which was nice. I loved moody weather from time to time, but today I was moody enough myself that I didn't need storm clouds added in. The breeze was slight and the lake calm. The dogs seemed to be having a blast running along the beach, chasing one another. Charlie hung back with me, as he always did. He was the smallest dog in a pack of large ones, so if he didn't hang back anyway, he might get trampled.

I was just rounding the house on our way back in when Zak pulled up. All eight dogs ran over to greet him, so I followed as well. Zak got out of the truck and began unloading groceries. I pitched in to help.

"I wasn't sure what type of dog food you'd want for the stray, so I got the kind for nursing mothers."

"That will be perfect. Alex thinks they'll be born today."

Zak climbed the steps to the kitchen door. "Still no word on the owner?"

"Not yet."

The others saw that Zak had groceries, and all, except Nona, who stayed behind to watch the babies, went out to the drive to help. It didn't take long for five people to empty the truck. Alex volunteered to put things away, and when Zak headed toward his office, I joined him. I thought it was important for us to stay on the same page, plus I knew he'd stopped off to speak to Salinger while he was out.

"So, did Salinger have any news?" I asked right away.

"Some. Sit down and I'll fill you in. I think between the two of us, we're getting a better grip on who the victim was, but so far that hasn't done us any good in identifying his killer, unless the killer's someone he knew from Los Angeles."

"Do you think that's the answer?" I wondered.

Zak shook his head. "Not necessarily, but we have to keep looking at every angle. Boris Grimly has to be our prime suspect at this point, but we haven't had any luck figuring out who he really is, so we're broadening our search parameters."

"It sounds like you and Salinger are working together."

"We are. I'm doing the computer stuff and he's doing the cop stuff."

I let out a little huff. "I feel kind of left out."

Zak grabbed my hand. "I knew you would, which is why I have a job for you."

Okay, now I was suspicious. "What kind of a job?"

"I need someone to call Edgar Irvine's agent pretending to be a writer looking for representation. Salinger already tried to get something out of him about why Irvine decided to come to Ashton Falls, but he wouldn't talk. As a perspective client, maybe you can get him to open up a bit."

"I'll do my best," I said. "Although I'm not sure how I'm going to work questions about Irvine into a conversation about possible representation. Maybe I'll just pretend to be a magazine editor writing a story. I can appeal to his desire for publicity."

"Whatever works." Zak smiled at me.

While I suspected this was a made-up job to get me to feel like I was helping when I really wasn't, Zoe Donovan Zimmerman could pull information out of even the most reluctant witness. By the time I finished my conversation with the agent, I knew Irvine hadn't come to Ashton Falls alone; he left Hollywood with his new girlfriend. I also found out that Irvine's ex-wife, who had demonstrated nothing but contempt for her ex recently, had moved to Bryton Lake a year ago, which meant she was plenty close enough to make the trip to town to kill him.

"Didn't you say Salinger told you the desk clerks at the inn saw Irvine coming and going on several different occasions?" Zak asked.

"He did tell me that, and no, in anticipation of your next question, he didn't say a thing about Irvine being with anyone. I suppose a call to the inn might be in order to verify that information. I'll add it to my list."

"I'll call the ex-wife," Zak offered. "I'll tell her I'm working as a consultant for the Ashton Falls Sheriff's Office and have a few questions. Did the agent know why Irvine came here?"

"It was just as we expected. He told his agent he got some tips on potential locations for future work and was taking a trip to check them out. He also made a comment about Irvine wanting to get new work in LA as soon as was possible. Something about a competitor." I looked at my notes. "He said the competitor was carving a niche for himself, and some of the producers he'd worked with in the past were looking at his work. The agent felt that might have been the reason Irvine responded to the tip in such an expedient manner. He wanted to keep the upper hand."

"Okay," Zak said. "I'll call the ex-wife and you call the inn to ask about the girlfriend."

By the time I made my call Zak was on the phone with Salinger, but I overheard enough of the conversation to know the ex-wife hadn't seen or spoken to Irvine and wasn't even aware he'd come to Ashton Falls or that he was dead. The clerk I spoke to verified that Irvine had checked in to the inn alone. If the agent was correct and Irvine left Hollywood with a woman, he was no longer with her when he arrived here. Of course, it was possible the woman might have been one of the assistants we knew he oftentimes hired rather than a girlfriend, and she might have found her own place to stay.

"What did Salinger want?" I asked when Zak hung up.

"The venom used to kill Edgar Irvine was extracted from an African black mamba."

"Okay. Is that important information?" I asked.

"It's one of the most poisonous snakes in the world, and it isn't found in the wild in North America, nor is it sold in this country," Zak answered. "At least not legally. There are always dealers who'll sell anything on the black market. Salinger found someone who'd heard of another black-market dealer, a competitor, who reportedly secured a black mamba for a client who asked to remain anonymous."

"So this guy who bought the snake has to be our killer."

"I won't say he *has to be*, but I do think it's possible, even likely, the person who bought the snake is the killer. The exchange took place on October 15."

"So the timeline fits." I frowned. "Sort of."

"It's feasible the killer bought this snake on October 15, extracted the venom, then used it to kill Edgar Irvine on October 22. And while I wouldn't necessarily consider the next piece of information a smoking gun, I do think it's interesting that this particular black-market deal went down at the Port of Los Angeles."

I paused. "So the killer bought this snake ten days ago in Los Angeles. The victim lived in Los Angeles and, as far as we know, was there when the venom was secured. So why lure him all the way to Ashton Falls? Why not just kill him in his home or where he worked?"

"There's more." Zak brought up a photo on his computer. "This is you, taken in front of Rosie's. I'd dropped you off and gone to park the car. You were supposed to go in and get a table, but you had a weird feeling and paused to look around."

"I remember. I felt like I was being watched."

"That night was October 15."

I was beginning to catch on. "So, the person who snapped the photo can't have been the same one who bought the snake. That means the person who killed Irvine didn't buy the snake, or the person who killed Irvine isn't stalking me, or the person who killed Irvine procured the venom and has been stalking me but had an accomplice who either took the photo or picked up the snake."

Zak nodded. "I think that about sums it up."

I sat back in my chair, stretching my legs out in front of me. "So which is it?"

He shrugged.

I let out a long groan. "So we're back to square one."

Zak put a hand on my arm. "We aren't rounding third base, but I think we're doing better than square one."

"That's a mixed metaphor," I pointed out.

Zak winked at me. "I know, but let's go with it."

"Okay, so what does this information really tell us?"

Zak turned back to his computer. "In isolation, not a lot. But we have information, even if it doesn't all fit together yet. In the end, the more information we have, the more likely we are to identify the killer."

"Why that snake?" I asked.

Zak raised a brow. "I don't follow."

"If your intention was to inject snake venom into a man, making it look as if he'd been bitten by a vampire, why extract venom from that snake? There are plenty of poisonous snakes right here in the United States. Rattlers come to mind. They're easy to find in nature and they'll make him just as dead. Why on earth would anyone go to all the trouble of importing a dangerous, lethal snake from Africa? I mean, the cost alone must have been astronomical. It's not like the person who sold the snake could have just put it in his carryon. I'm sure if the black-market dealer smuggled an illegal snake into the country he was going to want to be paid a lot for it."

"That's true," Zak said. "The cost of killing Irvine is going to weed out people such as his ex-wife or an overly enthusiastic competitor."

I cocked a grin. "So I guess the lead about the snake is already useful. I should never have doubted you. I really do feel we're beginning to develop a profile of the killer."

Zak narrowed his gaze. "Someone bent on killing who's not only crazy but rich and connected. Sure. That'll be an easy person to track down."

Chapter 8

"I think you're on to something with the *why this snake* thing," Zak said. "I wonder if Irvine had been to Africa in the past year or so."

"Can you find out?"

"Give me a minute to check passport entries and credit-card receipts. While I'm doing that, why don't you call Irvine's agent back to see if you can find out anything more about the woman he supposedly left Los Angeles with. A name would be helpful at the very least."

I watched Zak as he turned back to the computer. While I really, really hated the reason the two of us were sequestered in the lab working on a shared project, I was enjoying this time with him. It seemed as if life had gotten in the way of our relationship lately. Not that we were having any problems. It was more that we'd both been very busy with projects we worked on independently of each other. If there was one thing that had been coming through loud and clear the past few weeks, it was that despite the family we loved, Zak and I needed to carve out couple time.

The agent was able to tell me that the first name of the woman Irvine left Los Angeles with was Stella. He didn't know her last name. He also said Irvine had been on edge recently. I asked when he thought the nervousness had begun, and he thought it was around the time he returned from an overseas trip to do research on a novel he was working on that included several paranormal phenomena, including a ghost at the Parthenon, a disappearing mountain in Siberia, and an otherworld portal in the Serengeti.

"Are any of those actual things?" Zak asked when I filled him in.

"The agent didn't think so, but he didn't seem to care much. Irvine's books have sold well and they were marketed as fiction, so he didn't have the burden of proving anything one way or the other."

"So if he was researching paranormal phenomena in the Serengeti he might have made a trip to Africa," Zak said.

I nodded. "I guess he might have. Have you found out where he went yet?"

"Working on it."

I took a few minutes to check on the kids. Scooter was in his room reading the latest sci-fi thriller he'd picked up in the library, Alex was laying on her bed talking on the phone, and Catherine was downstairs in the living room with Ellie, Eli, Mom, and Harper.

"How's it going?" Mom asked.

I shrugged my shoulders. "We're picking up clues as we go, but so far nothing is really coming together."

"We were thinking of going for a walk along the lakeshore," Mom said. "Would you like to come with us? Some fresh air might do you good."

I hesitated. I'd told Zak I'd stay around the house, but fresh air might really help. "I'd like to. Let me tell Zak what I'm doing. I'll grab the sand stroller for Eli and Catherine. The older kids might want to come along too, if only to get out of the house, so I'll let them know too."

Ellie offered to change both babies and Mom rounded up the dogs. It was a beautiful autumn day, the leaves along the shore in full color. It would be nice to get outside and appreciate all the lake had to offer. I knew Zak was concerned for my safety, but if the adage that there was safety in numbers was true, I was in good shape within the large group that set off along the water's edge.

"I can't believe Haunted Hamlet is this weekend," Ellie said. "In the past I would have been knee-deep in volunteer duties. It feels odd to take on the role of spectator, although with a toddler who's into everything and a baby on the way, I don't see how I could have committed to doing anything this weekend."

"I haven't been the one to organize the zombie run. I'm sure the woman Hillary got to take it over will do a fine job, but I'm struggling with being on the sidelines."

The pack of dogs came running back as Shep, who had been the one to retrieve the stick I'd tossed, dropped it at my feet. I picked it up and threw it again, and all the dogs, other than Charlie, took off after it.

"It's natural to want to ease back into things after having a baby," Ellie said. "With baby number two on the way, I'm thinking of quitting the events committee altogether. I go to the meetings, but I don't contribute much. I think it might be better for the others to find someone to replace me who's willing to chair events and spearhead volunteer duties."

Ellie had a point. The events committee was very hands-on. Sure, there were a lot of volunteers in the community besides the ten of us, but it was usually one of the ten who was the chairperson. Before we had children, Ellie and I had chaired several events every year.

"It would seem odd to be off the committee completely," I said, "but I see what you're saying." I glanced at my mom. "You're the one person in this town not on the committee who really should be. You have tons of experience organizing events, and Harper will be going to kindergarten next year, so you'll have time."

Mom's expression grew thoughtful. "I might think about taking on something like that. Who would I talk to if I were interested?"

"Hillary Spain. Trust me, she'll be thrilled to have you."

When we returned home from our walk, I learned Zak had used the time to track down Stella. He'd begun by doing a search linking the name *Edgar Irvine* with her name and found out he'd lived near a Stella Applewood and occasionally spent time with her. Zac tracked down a cell phone number for her and called it. Stella had flown here with Irvine, but when they arrived at the airport in Bryton Lake, she'd been picked up by a sister who lived nearby, while he rented a car and continued on to Ashton Falls.

Stella hadn't heard Irvine was dead and was quite upset when Zak let the news slip. After she calmed down a bit, he managed to convince her to let us come to her sister's place in Bryton Lake to ask her a few questions. Zak was ready to go, so I quickly got cleaned up to join him. Mom and Ellie were fine with keeping an eye on Catherine.

"Did she tell you anything on the phone other than that she was staying with her sister?" I asked as Zak sped down the mountain.

"She didn't say a lot, just that she lived near Irvine and they were friends. When he talked about his trip to Ashton Falls, she told him that she had a sister in Bryton Lake. She'd been thinking about making a trip anyway, and coming at the same time would be company for the flight. Apparently, she hates to fly alone."

"But she hadn't heard that Irvine had been killed?"

"No, and she was understandably upset. I didn't go into any detail, just said his body was found in one of the haunted places he was here to research. I'm hoping she'll know something about his trip to Africa, and whether he was having issues with anyone in his life."

Stella had pulled herself together by the time we arrived at her sister's home. She offered us coffee, then suggested we take chairs around the kitchen table. Initially, she had questions for us, which we answered to the best of our ability, and then she agreed to answer ours.

"I understand Mr. Irvine went on a research trip six months ago," Zak began.

"Yes, that's correct. He had work to do on several projects. He was supposed to be gone for six weeks, but his assistant, Becka, died while they were away, so he came home two weeks early."

"Do you know how she died?" Zak asked.

"Snakebite. There are some nasty snakes in Africa. From what Edgar told me, they'd been camping out on the Serengeti and Becka wandered away from the camp. She was dead when Edgar found her."

"That's so tragic," I said.

Stella lifted a shoulder. "If you ask me, Becka was a bit of a loose cannon. She was very young, barely out of college, really. From what I heard from some of the other assistants Edgar worked with, she ignored the safety protocol Edgar had set up. In the course of his work, he sometimes put himself in dangerous situations. Edgar was careful, but Becka wasn't. I don't know why he didn't cut her loose and get someone better suited."

I couldn't be sure, but I felt I was picking up on some jealousy here. Maybe the two women had been in competition for Irvine's attention.

"Was Becka close to anyone who might have blamed Irvine for her death?" Zak asked.

"You think someone killed Edgar because they were upset that she died while on the trip with him?"

"It's an idea," Zak answered.

Stella paused to think about it. Eventually, she said, "There *was* this one guy, Matt. I know he blamed Edgar for both seducing Becka and for being careless and getting her killed." She tapped her finger to her chin. "Matt Carson. I think he must have been one of her exes."

"Matt was angry that Edgar seduced Becka? Were they having a physical relationship?" I asked.

"They were doing it around the clock."

Okay, I didn't need that degree of detail. I found it a little odd that Irvine had attracted a much younger woman. Of course, some women went for older guys. I wrinkled my nose and moved on from this train of thought. "How long had they been a couple before the trip?"

"A few months, I guess. Might have been less. Edgar didn't discuss his sex life with me, but I knew when he was getting some."

"Do you think this Matt Carson was mad enough to kill him?" Zak asked.

"Heck yeah. The guy was on a rampage. I'm pretty sure he might have killed Edgar then and there when he tracked him down if we hadn't been in a public place and I hadn't been with him. Though I didn't get the vibe he would set up a fancy murder. I called Edgar's agent after I spoke to you," she nodded her head toward Zac, "and he filled me in on the details. If Edgar had been shot in the streets of LA, I'd say Matt was your man."

"Can you think of anyone who might have wanted Edgar dead who *would* have gone to the trouble and expense of setting up a murder by snake venom?" I asked.

Stella screwed up her mouth. "I suppose it could have been one of his cult friends."

"Cult friends?" I asked.

"Edgar was in this group in LA. It's really nothing more than a bunch of kooks who are in to role-playing. They take on personas and dress and act like their characters."

"Characters? Like vampires?" I wondered.

Stella nodded. "Vampires, zombies, werewolves, and other creatures of the night. I'm not in to that whole vibe, so I've never been to one of their events, but I know they get together a few times a month and play dress-up. One of the guys even had actual vampire fangs implanted. I mean, that seems way over the top. It's not like he can pop them off and on; they're permanent. There are a lot of role-playing groups around the country, but this particular one is very exclusive, and I know the members spend a lot of money on costumes and props. And when I say a lot, I mean like enough to buy a freaking house." Stella rolled her eyes. "Pretty nuts."

It seemed likely at least a few of the people who'd descended on Ashton Falls were associated with that group.

"I don't suppose you can give us the names of anyone who might have more insight into the group?" I asked. "Maybe someone you know is a member."

"I guess Edgar's friend Spider might talk to you. I think he spent some time with the group at one point, although I don't know that he was a regular."

"Does Spider have a real name?" Zak asked.

"Probably, but I don't know what it is. Spider and Edgar used to hang out in an old blues bar downtown. I think it's called Poor Daddy's. Someone there might know."

Chapter 9

By the time we got home it was time to start thinking about dinner. Levi was knee-deep in football season, so I figured he wouldn't be wrapping up until around five. My dad closed Donovan's then, and the rest of us were already here. I supposed if we planned dinner for six we could accommodate everyone. There was another storm predicted for the weekend, but tonight was beautiful. I was tempted to suggest a BBQ on the deck. The sun would have set by the time we started eating, but we had a large fire pit, several deck heaters, and plenty of lights if you counted not only the patio lights and the thousands of orange and white twinkle lights Zak had strung. Thursday was usually my book club night, and I was sorry to miss it, but I'd promised to stay home.

"How about burgers on the deck?" I asked everyone gathered in the living room discussing their plans for the upcoming holiday season.

"Sounds good," Ellie said. "I can make a potato salad."

"And I'll make a fruit salad," Mom offered.

"I figure it'll be around six if we wait for Dad and Levi, but it should be a warm evening, and we have the fire pit and heaters."

"It'll be like a fairyland with all Zak's lights," Nona added.

"That's what I thought." I smiled. "And it might be our last chance for a while. I heard there's a storm blowing in tomorrow, to be followed by a cold front. I'm going to call Salinger and check in; then I'll check on Alex and Scooter. I assume Catherine is napping."

"Yes, but both babies should be up shortly," Ellie informed me.

With our plans for dinner firmed up, I headed upstairs to call Salinger. He didn't answer, so I left a message, then went to see the kids.

Scooter was laying on his bed, tossing a football into the air, catching it, and tossing it again.

"Something wrong, buddy?" I asked.

"Nothing's wrong, but I decided not to go to the dance."

I sat down on the edge of the bed. "I thought you were looking forward to it."

"I was," Scooter said as he tossed the ball extra high.

"What mind you change your mind?"

Scooter shrugged.

"Did you have a fight with Tucker?" While they'd been best friends for a lot of years, the boys got into spats every now and then.

"No, Tucker and I are cool."

I paused, trying to work this out. Scooter hadn't been planning to go to the dance with a date, but that didn't mean he hadn't tried to get one. "Does your change of heart have to do with a girl?"

Scooter shrugged again.

I just kept guessing to see where it got me. "You decided to ask someone other than Tucker to go with you?"

"Lacy Martin."

"Lacy Martin?"

"She's just a girl in my English class. We hang out sometimes. I guess you could say we're friends."

"So you asked Lacy to go with you and she said no?"

"She said her dad was real strict and wouldn't let her date, but she was going to the dance with a friend, and maybe she'd see me there. That's when I asked Tucker. I figured we could go together and Lacy would go with her friend, and we'd meet up."

"That sounds like a good plan."

"It was, until I found out Lacy was going to the dance with a date after all. Danny Green. I called and asked her about it, and she said she talked to her dad and got him to change his mind about the no-date thing."

"I see. I'm so sorry. I know that must make you feel bad."

Scooter continued to toss the ball. Normally, I'd suggest he find someone else to go with, but given the situation, it might be best if he did stay home. "If you want to go I think you should go with Tucker like you planned. I'm sure there will be girls there without dates who'd welcome the opportunity to dance. But if you definitely don't want to go maybe Tucker can come here and spend the night. You guys can set up in the den and watch Halloween movies and eat popcorn."

"Can we get pizza?"

"Absolutely."

"And it will be just me and Tucker? Everyone else will have to stay out?"

"If that's what you want."

Scooter's face grew thoughtful. "I'll ask him. I was looking forward to the dance, but having a sleepover sounds good too."

Sometimes it amazed me how different Scooter and Alex were. Socially, I would say he was slightly behind the curve for kids his age in terms of things like girls and dating. I supposed the fact that he had a girl he liked and wanted to take to the dance showed he was maturing, but he was still at a point where he could be easily distracted by monster movies and video games. Alex, though, who had already been in high school for a couple of years, felt almost like a young adult to me. The two still got along really well, which I was delighted about, but their interests had most certainly deviated.

After I'd settled things with Scooter, I went in to see Alex, who was sitting at her desk working on a complicated-looking mathematical equation. "What are you doing?"

"My homework. I had Phyllis e-mail everything to me so I wouldn't get behind. Hazel's going to stop by later to drop off some material she gathered on the Norlander mine. I really want to go out and take a look at the place. Reading and research is fine, but a firsthand experience will be better."

"I'll talk to Zak about it. Maybe he can take you. Is Hazel coming by tonight?"

Alex nodded. "She said she'd come by after she closes the library. She asked if I thought you were going to make it to book club. If you were she was going to give it to you then, but I said you probably wouldn't."

"That was nice of her. Did she find anything interesting?"

Alex stopped what she was doing and looked up. "Yes. The Norlanders had a sister, Amelia, who lived with them and kept house for them while they worked the mine. After the brothers died she stayed in Devil's Den. Hazel told me she married and raised a family there. After all the mines closed and everyone left, she and her husband claimed some acreage and lived off the land."

"Wow. That is interesting. I'd like to hear the rest of the story once you work out the details." I glanced at my phone, which had begun to vibrate. "It's Salinger. I should take this. BBQ on the patio at about six."

I walked out into the hall before answering the phone. "Hi, Salinger. Thanks for returning my call. I'm really just looking for an update."

"I have one, but I think it would be best to deliver it in person. Is Zak there with you?"

"I'm upstairs and he's downstairs in the computer room, but yeah, he's here."

"Okay. I'll be right over."

******

When Salinger arrived we all went into the computer room. He pulled a photo out of an envelope and said, "I've been going through all the photos in the box you found to see if I noticed anything that might be construed as a clue. I found this." He handed the photo to me.

It was me, walking past a large delivery truck. "Okay. So?"

"If you look closely you can see your image reflected in the aluminum siding."

I looked closer. Salinger was right; you could see my image. You could also see someone else's. "The man who took the photo."

"Exactly."

Zak walked up next to me and looked at the photo as well. It wasn't a great photo. The guy had on a baseball cap and the large digital camera was being held in front of his face.

"It would help if we could see his face," I said. I turned to Salinger. "This was a good catch, but I don't think it tells us anything."

"Sure it does. The photographer appears to be male, so if we go with that assumption, we eliminate about half the population. The lab was able to determine the photographer is five feet ten to eleven inches, which eliminates everyone either taller or shorter than that. He's of average weight, maybe one seventy to one seventy-five, so that eliminates people who are under- or overweight. His hair is short and the cap covers most of it, but there's enough showing at the bottom of the cap to tell us it's brown. If you look at the hand holding the camera, you can see a few liver spots, so he isn't very young, but it doesn't appear to be that of a man over fifty either. My lab estimates the hand belongs to someone between thirty-five and forty-five."

"That still leaves a lot of people," Zak pointed out.

"It does," Salinger agreed. "Now let's narrow down when the photo was taken."

I studied the image and tried to place it. "I have on my fuzzy orange sweater," I said. "I only wear it at this time of the year, and I only dug it out of my storage chest a few weeks ago, so the photo was taken within the past three weeks." I paused and looked at the area around me. "It looks like I'm in the parking lot at the grocery store. Zak does the weekly shopping, but I pop in for milk and diapers and stuff. Given the orange sweater and the fact that Catherine isn't with me, I'm going to say this photo was taken when I stopped by for diapers after the events committee meeting the Wednesday before last."

Salinger was jotting down notes. "Time you were there?"

"I guess around noon."

Salinger closed his notebook. "Okay, now that we know when and where the photo was taken, I'll start asking around to see if anyone remembers seeing a guy standing in the parking lot taking photos. It's not normal behavior. I bet someone took note of it."

Wow, maybe Salinger really did have something.

"I know you can't see the guy's face," Zak said, "but something about him is familiar."

I looked at the photo again. "Yeah. I had the same feeling. It's like I can almost recognize him, but there isn't quite enough there to connect all the dots."

"It might help if you both went through the box of photos to try to create a timeline," Salinger said. "Sort them by date taken. Try to identify where the photos were taken. Maybe Zoe will remember seeing something. We sometimes catch a glimpse of something, though it doesn't really register. Still, the image is buried in our subconscious, just waiting for someone or something to jar it loose."

"Do you have the box with you?" I asked.

Salinger handed me the envelope he'd been carrying. "I made copies of the best ones. Start with these to see if we can figure out who this guy is."

That, I decided, would make my life a whole lot easier.

Salinger left, and Zak and I sorted through the photos. It was giving me the creeps that this guy had photos taken in so many of the places I'd been in recent weeks. It seemed to me if someone had been following me frequently I would have noticed I had a tail. The fact that I hadn't suspected a thing was causing me concern. Sure, it looked as if a lot of the photos had been taken with a telephoto lens, but still. I couldn't believe my Zodar hadn't kicked in to warn me that something was up.

"You know what strikes me as I look at these photos?" I said to Zak. "Their randomness. None of the photos seem particularly important. Most were taken as I walked through parking lots, crossed streets, walked the dogs, shopped for diapers. They don't seem to have been taken to prove something or to tell a story. They don't seem to reveal anything important or a pattern. So why bother to take them in the first place?"

"I guess your stalker might have wanted to demonstrate he had eyes on you wherever you were at whatever time of the day."

"Okay, say that's true. Say my stalker wanted to prove to me that he could watch me at any time, in any place. Why make the photos so hard to find? I feel like I was led to the basement at Henderson House specifically to find the body of Edgar Irvine, but the photos were hidden in the loft of the barn, where it was entirely possible no one would ever find them. If the purpose of taking the photos was to scare me, why not plaster them to the walls of the basement? Because I have to tell you, if I had found these plastered to the walls at the same time I found the body, it would have scared the bejeezus out of me."

Zak's expression turned to a scowl. "You make a good point. On one hand, the fact that the photos were stored in the loft certainly didn't guarantee the photographer they'd be found, if that was his intention, but the loft also wouldn't be a good choice for a storage location if the stalker didn't want them found."

"So why were they there? And how long had they been there? And does the fact that they were in the barn indicate in any way that my stalker has been spending a lot of time there? Is he camping there? I didn't see evidence of a camper, but there was an old mattress in the attic that wasn't there when I was last at the house."

Zak groaned. "There really isn't a single thing about this that makes a lick of sense. The only consistency I've found at all is that there doesn't seem to be any rhyme or reason to any of it."

I sat on the floor and began to create a timeline with the photos. "I think we might want to consider that the photographs were taken by someone other than the vampire killer. It seems like the person who killed Irvine must be in some way linked to his life. Maybe it's someone who blames him for Becka's death, or it's one of his weird cult buddies. The use of the serum from an African black mamba seems too specific not to be relevant. And it does seem like Irvine was intentionally lured here. But these photos of me seem random and unfocused. Even the choice of a storage place makes it seem as if the stalker wasn't sure whether he wanted the photos to be found or not. I'm not getting the vibe that the person who meticulously planned out and executed the elaborate murder at Henderson House is the same one behind this hodgepodge of photos."

"But there's one common variable," Zak said. "You. Both the killer and the stalker seemed weirdly interested in you."

I supposed Zak could be right, but the longer I looked at the photos, the more certain I was that they were taken by an amateur, not a methodical killer who'd lure a man to a small town where, as far I as I knew, he'd never been before, only to kill him using a fanglike contraption to deliver venom from a black-market snake that happened to be the same kind that had killed his assistant. And then there was the fact that he not only got the media involved but managed to maneuver me to the same house on the same day. The man who killed Irvine knew what he was doing and had most likely killed before.

Chapter 10

Friday, October 26

"How'd you sleep?" Nona asked the following morning, after I dragged myself to the kitchen table, where Zak had a cup of coffee waiting for me.

"I didn't sleep." I yawned. "At least not much. I have a feeling there's a nap in my future."

"I think a nap is a good idea," Zak said. "In fact, you should probably plan to stay in today. I'd feel better if you didn't leave the house at all."

I wanted to argue but figured that could wait. Changing the subject, I said, "Where are the kids?"

"Catherine is still sleeping and the older two are upstairs," Zak answered.

I frowned. "Seems late for Catherine to still be sleeping."

"I checked on her a couple of times and she seemed to be sleeping peacefully. I'll see if I can wake her in a little while if she doesn't get up on her own."

I took a sip of my coffee but didn't reply one way or the other.

"I'm going back to my suite to shower," Nona said. She took her mug and plate to the sink. "I have a doctor's appointment in Bryton Lake, so I'll be gone until late this afternoon."

"Do you need a ride?" Zak asked.

"No. A friend is taking me. We're going to do some shopping after my appointment and maybe have some lunch. Make a day of it."

"That sounds like fun," Zak replied. "Do you need some money?"

Nona looked insulted. "No, I don't need any money. I'm a grown woman. I can pay for my own expenses."

Zak offered a sheepish grin. "I'm sorry. I guess I'm just used to asking the kids if they need money."

Nona's face softened. "I'm sorry I snapped at you. I should have realized. I'm just having a cranky day. A trip down the mountain will do me good."

After I'd had my coffee, I headed upstairs to get dressed. I peeked in on Catherine, who was still fast asleep. It wasn't unheard of for her to sleep this late, but it didn't happen very often. If she was still sleeping by the time I was dressed I'd gently wake her. I knew from experience it wasn't a good idea to allow her routine to become too skewed if I didn't want an unhappy infant on my hands.

It looked to be a cooler day today, so I chose jeans and a sweatshirt. I pulled my hair into a ponytail, then went to wake my sleeping princess.

"Good morning, sweetie," I said in a soft voice as I slowly lifted the blind.

Catherine rolled over but didn't open her eyes. I put a hand on her forehead. She felt cool, so it didn't seem as if she had a fever.

"It's time to get up and have some breakfast," I said, gently rubbing her stomach.

One eye opened and then the other.

"Are you hungry? Daddy made pancakes."

Catherine sat up and looked at me. "Da."

"Daddy's in his office. How about we get you dressed?"

Catherine reached out her arms and I picked her up. I kissed the top of her curly hair before I carried her to the changing table and laid her down. I handed her a dolly to hold while I changed her diaper and dressed her in a warm outfit. Then I picked her up and took her downstairs. I was halfway there when Zak appeared at the bottom.

"Da," Catherine screeched, almost squirming out of my arms.

"There's my girl." Zak smiled. I carefully transferred my little daddy's girl into his arms and followed them into the kitchen. "I think I may have found something," he informed me. "Let's feed this little munchkin, then we can discuss it."

I really hated it when Zak opened the door to a conversation that sounded intriguing, then made me wait for the rest of it, but Catherine did need to be fed, and I didn't want to discuss an unpleasant subject, like death, while she was within hearing range, even if she couldn't understand what we were saying.

Once again, I changed the subject. "I wanted to talk to you about the dance at the Academy," I dove in, thinking this was as good a time as any to address it. "I know you don't want the kids leaving the house, and I support that, but Alex has worked hard on her costume and has been looking forward to the evening. I'd like to discuss an option where she can follow through with her plans."

Zak sat down across from Catherine and began feeding her the homemade baby food he added to the pancakes she loved. "I don't disagree with you. I've thought about the dance as well. I guess it would be okay to let her go, within a few parameters."

"Such as?" I took a sip of my coffee.

"I drive her to and from the dance. I walk her in and she waits for me to escort her back to the car afterward. I'm fine with picking Diego up so they can arrive together. And we notify the dance chaperones of the situation, so they can keep an eye on things."

I let out a breath. Whew. That was easier than I'd expected. "I think she'll agree to that. I honestly thought you were going to want to go on her date with her."

"I *do* want to go on Alex's date with her." Zak smiled. "But I won't. She's a smart, capable girl. I'm confident she can avoid putting herself into a dangerous situation even if her honorary mother has often found that task impossible to accomplish."

"I've been staying out of trouble just fine lately," I shot back. I wanted to elaborate but decided it was best to leave well enough alone. "I'm going to let Alex know about the dance while you finish feeding Catherine. We can talk after."

"Are Ellie and your mother coming over again?" Zak asked.

"Yes. They should both be here soon. I know it isn't an ideal situation, but I feel better having them here when Levi and Dad are at work, rather than having them home alone with just Eli and Harper."

I headed to Alex's bedroom, where I found her sitting on the floor watching the newborn puppies, who were curled up with their mama in the closet.

"How's the little family doing today?" I asked.

"Good. All four pups seem healthy and they're all eating. The mama dog is pretty tired after her ordeal, but she's eating and drinking, so I think she'll be fine. How are you doing?"

I shrugged. "I'm okay. I wish this thing was over with, of course. I just spoke with Zak, who's fine with you going to the dance. There are a few rules you'll need to follow, but he isn't even planning to go along with you, so that shows progress."

Alex smiled. "It does. I promise to follow the rules and stay out of trouble. Are Ellie and Grandma coming over again today?"

"Yes. They should be here soon."

"Good. I wanted to talk to them about my makeup. I won't need much, but I want some. Grandma said she'd help me figure out the best look for my character."

I chatted with Alex for a while longer, then went back downstairs. I could hear Ellie and my mom talking to Zak in the kitchen. Again I felt guilt wash over me. If not for me they'd be going about their everyday lives.

******

We got Catherine settled in Zak's office. I was curious to hear what he had to say and hoped it would be something that would make sense of everything. I really, really wanted to get back to enjoying what was left of Halloween.

"So what do you have?" I asked him after I'd pulled up a chair and sat down next to him. When he worked he was usually in the zone. I wasn't even sure he'd seen me sit down next to him.

Zak ran a hand through his blond hair, which had grown long and thick on the top. "First, I managed to convince Carl Poland to come clean about the thousand-dollar-a-month payment Irvine had been sending him. It seems he's in possession of something that proves Irvine was responsible for Becka's death. He was blackmailing him."

I frowned. "I thought Becka died as the result of a snakebite."

"She did, but according to Poland, it was Irvine who told Becka to approach the snake so he could get a photo. After she died Irvine acted like he hadn't been anywhere nearby, that Becka had broken protocol and wandered off on her own. Poland admitted he wasn't on the trip, so he didn't have firsthand evidence of what happened, but while he was searching in Irvine's files for a source he needed for his current research project, he found a document written by Irvine admitting the truth. Poland realized the value of the information and decided to use it to help his bottom line."

"He wouldn't have killed Irvine if he was benefiting from Irvine's mistake. Did he have any idea who might have wanted him dead?"

"No. I mentioned the guy Stella brought up, Matt Carson. Poland had heard about the altercation he'd had with Irvine, but he thought a shot to the head in a dark alley would be more his style. He was sure Carson wouldn't have come up with the whole vampire thing. He did say Becka had a brother who was part of the role-playing group Irvine belonged to, thought his name was Mark or Mitch or something like that. Someone else I spoke to thought his first name could be Mason, and she said Becka's last name was Watson. Poland never met the brother and didn't know what he looked like, but he'd heard the guy was loaded. If the brother blamed Irvine for his sister's death, was in to the dress-up thing, and had the financial means to procure the venom, he might be a viable suspect."

"Salinger is looking in to the brother as well. We figure with all the vampires in town now, someone visiting from the LA group might know who a member with a sister named Becka might be."

"That's great, Zak. This feels like the first real lead we've had. This guy would have the motive to want Irvine dead and he could afford to kill him the same way his sister died, though I still don't know why he'd go to all the trouble of staging the murder in Ashton Falls or what he has to do with me."

Zak frowned. "Yeah, that part still isn't clear."

"Do you have anything else?"

"I followed up with several other people who've worked as assistants to Irvine. Most agreed he was an okay boss. He paid them all an hourly rate for research, transcription, data processing, or whatever else he needed. He was a nice-enough guy, although he was a bit of a womanizer; it seems Becka wasn't the only female assistant he had a physical relationship with. Several of the other assistants told me he traveled frequently, and it wasn't unheard of for him to take one or more of them with him. It was considered a perk by most. I asked about Becka specifically, and it did seem it was widely known they'd become a couple, though according to the rumor mill, Irvine had been thinking about breaking up with her. In fact, one of Irvine's ex-assistants said the only reason he hadn't dumped her before the trip to Africa was because he had a social relationship with Becka's brother and didn't want to upset that particular apple cart."

"Did anyone say they'd heard Irvine might have been responsible for Becka's death?"

Zak shook his head. "I don't think that's a conclusion anyone other than Poland, who found the document, would necessarily have come to."

"Have you spent any time checking out Becka?"

"I did a search for Rebecca Watson of Los Angeles and found some basic information on her. I haven't done an extensive search yet, but it appears she'd never been married, so it seems the brother's last name could be Watson as well. I'll look for information about Mark or Mitch or Mason Watson and see what I can find. If nothing pops I'll try to find a link to a brother by digging further into Becka's records."

I smiled. "I feel like we might actually be getting somewhere. I know we still don't have a smoking gun, but I feel like we're making progress. How can I help?"

"We never did finish our timeline last night. I'm not sure it's relevant, but Salinger thought it important enough to ask us to do it. I'll continue with my search if you want to work on that."

I doubted developing a timeline was anything more than busy work, but I went along with it for now. Zak had been pretty accommodating when it came to supporting my involvement on any level, so I didn't want to make things complicated for him by being difficult. I figured if I hung out in the background, as Zak wanted, when things got down to the real nitty-gritty I'd have a front-row seat at the takedown.

Before I agreed to dig into the timeline I logged onto my e-mail account. There were several messages from Hillary that I'd deal with later. I also saw I had a return e-mail from Orson Spalding, the man who'd stopped by the Zoo looking for me the other day. He was in town to film an episode of *Monster Hunter* and wanted to know if I could meet him at the old cemetery outside of town. He'd been told I was the one to find the victim of the vampire killer and wanted to interview me about what I'd seen.

"Oh, this can't be a coincidence," I said aloud.

Chapter 11

"What can't be a coincidence?" Zak asked.

I looked up to find him staring at me. I explained about the man who'd spoken to Jeremy about me, and the e-mail I'd sent him to establish contact. My belief had been that he probably wanted to adopt a pet, I said, though the e-mail I'd just read had informed me otherwise.

"Call Salinger," Zak said as soon as I brought him up to speed.

I punched in Salinger's number. "Way ahead of you."

I waited while the phone rang, hoping Salinger would answer. This could be the break we needed. Or not. This case was so screwy, I was at the point where I wasn't certain what could be connected and what couldn't.

"Hey, Zoe. What's up," Salinger picked up after the fourth ring.

"We need to get out to the old graveyard outside of town right away."

"Why?"

I explained about the e-mail.

"Did he say when he wants to meet you?" Salinger asked.

"He said he'd be at the cemetery for most of the day. He hoped I'd get the message and stop by."

"I agree the e-mail should be checked out, but I think I should go alone. You're supposed to be hanging back where, theoretically at least, you'll be safe," Salinger reminded me.

"Zak is here and is willing to come with me, and you'll be with us. We should be perfectly safe."

Salinger hesitated.

"The guy wants to speak to me. In fact, it seems as if he's gone out of his way to speak to me specifically. We aren't sure if he'd be willing to talk to you or anyone else. He said he's in town to track down the vampire. He's a professional monster hunter, so he might know something important."

Salinger still hesitated. I plowed ahead. "I'm going to e-mail him back to say I'm on my way. Zak and I will meet you at the graveyard in twenty to twenty-five minutes."

"Let me come by to pick you both up," Salinger suggested. "It won't take that long for me to swing by your place, and we can discuss things on the drive over."

"Okay. We'll be ready."

As soon as I hung up the phone I headed downstairs to let the others know what we were doing. Mom offered to keep an eye on Catherine while we were gone. Levi was coming over to the house after work and my mom was going to call my dad to have him come here when he closed the store.

There was comfort in numbers; it seemed everyone was fine with hanging out here.

After Salinger picked us up I tried to quell my nerves by looking at the scenery out my window. I really loved this time of year, when everything was so fresh and colorful. I just hoped we could put the rest of the pieces of this mystery together and catch whoever had killed Irvine so I could stop thinking about it. Although by now I doubted that was true. I also hoped the same man who killed Irvine would turn out to be my stalker, so I could stop thinking about that too.

"You said you were going to e-mail this guy to let him know you were on your way," Salinger said. "Did he respond?"

I frowned. "No. Hopefully, he was just busy taking photos and whatnot and didn't have the opportunity to reply."

"Did he give you his cell phone number as well as his e-mail address?" Zak asked.

"No, just the e-mail address. Which is actually kind of odd. Most people have smartphones these days. When I e-mailed him I gave him my cell number and suggested he call or text, but he chose not to." I shrugged. "Different strokes for different folks, I guess."

Salinger turned off the main highway going out of town onto the county road off which the cemetery was located. "And you said he has a television show?"

"That's what he said, though I've never seen it. It's called *Monster Hunter*. You know," I said, "Jeremy said the guy looked familiar but couldn't place him. I wonder if he's seen the show and just didn't make the connection."

"Call him and ask."

I did as Salinger suggested. As it turned out, Jeremy *had* seen the show, and now that I mentioned it, he was sure the man who'd come in looking for me was the same person he'd watched tackle legendary creatures like Bigfoot and the Lake Tahoe Monster. Not that he'd managed to film either creature during the course of thirty-minute episodes, but he filmed on location where sightings had been reported and interviewed people who'd made them. According to Jeremy, the show was big on theatrics but short on content. Still, he said, it was entertaining.

"So he's here to try to capture the vampire on film?" Zak asked, a slight look of confusion on his face.

"That's what he indicated, although if that's his intention it seems he ought to be filming in the graveyard after dark. I guess he might have gone there early to do the groundwork."

"I could see how it would be important to get the lay of the land before setting up equipment for the shoot," Zak replied. "But there are several cemeteries in this area. I wonder why he honed in on this one."

"If I was looking for a vampire this is the cemetery I'd go to," I said. "It's the oldest. And I don't think anyone has been buried here in three quarters of a century or more, so there are seldom any visitors, and it has all those crypts. The newer cemetery in Ashton Falls doesn't have any of those, and the older one in town only has a few."

"If a vampire did want to set up camp in Ashton Falls I suppose this one would be the place to hang out in terms of isolation," Zak said, a hint of teasing in his voice. "Still, there wouldn't be much of a food source all the way out there. There are a lot more people in town, so there's more blood to dine on."

Were we seriously discussing vampires and their likely choice of lodging and food supply? This was getting crazier and crazier. "Look. There's a van in the dirt lot," I pointed out. "It must belong to Orson Spalding."

Salinger pulled up next to the van and we all got out. Salinger looked in the van's windows, but there was no one inside. There was a lot of expensive video equipment inside, which seemed to confirm its owner. A quick look around the cemetery, however, didn't reveal the person who went with it.

"I wonder where he went," I said.

"This is a big cemetery, and the crypts block our line of sight," Zak pointed out. "Let's just walk around and see if he pops up. I doubt he went far from all that equipment in the van."

Zak was right; the guy wouldn't have wandered far. There was an old abandoned house at the far side of the cemetery he might have decided to check out. It was totally trashed, but it was old and decrepit enough it would draw the attention of someone with monster hunting on his mind.

We wandered the grounds from one end to the other before we checked out the house, which was boarded up and locked, so it wasn't as if we could just wander inside. But if our monster hunter had found a way in, I reasoned, we could use the same one to look for him.

The front door was locked and the windows on that side all had large sheets of plywood nailed over them. The house was two stories, but from a visual inspection they didn't appear to have been tampered with. We walked around one side to the back, which looked to also be tightly buttoned up. It was on the far side of the house, where the branches of a large tree grew right up to the second story that we spotted an unboarded window that looked as if it might be cracked open.

"I can climb up," I offered.

"It's a pretty big climb," Salinger said.

"I'll go," Zak insisted.

"No, it has to be me," I countered. "The window's tiny. It's probably for a bathroom. Neither of you will fit through it."

"If we can't fit the monster hunter probably couldn't fit either," Salinger reasoned.

"Maybe not, but I'd hate to leave without knowing for sure whether he's inside." I looked around. "He has to be somewhere."

"Maybe we should just go back to the van and wait for him there," Zak suggested.

"It'll just take a minute for me to check," I argued.

"It could be a trap," Zak said.

Salinger looked back toward the cemetery grounds, assessing the situation. "I agree with Zak that the open window feels like a trap. I don't think Zoe should go in alone."

"Let's try prying one of the boards covering a downstairs window free," I suggested instead.

"The small window on the side did look like it might have been tampered with at some point," Zak said. "The board might be loose."

It took the three of us a few minutes to pry the board loose, and the window behind it wasn't locked, allowing us all access to the house's interior.

"This place is a mess," I said to no one in particular when we'd climbed through the window and entered the main living area. The year we'd tried to use it for Haunted Hamlet a man had died inside, and the person who'd killed him had vandalized it to cover his tracks.

"Hello," Zak called out as we walked through the dimly lit house.

"Mr. Spalding," I shouted. "Are you in here?"

No answer to either of us. We walked down the narrow hallway to the stairs to the second floor, pausing to look into each empty room. Once we'd cleared both the first and second level we headed back down the stairs and out the window in which we'd climbed.

"I didn't really think there'd be anyone in there," Salinger said.

"I know, but I'm glad we looked. At least now I won't wonder. What now?" I asked.

"Let's take another look around the cemetery. Maybe check the van again."

"Do you think the guy could be in one of the crypts? Maybe he's looking for a new coffin, or one that looks like it's been opened recently. If there's a new vampire in town a monster hunter would be looking for an empty coffin."

Salinger shrugged. "He could be in one of the crypts. Some are just small structures built up around a single coffin, but others are quite large. We can walk around them. If any of them were entered recently we should find evidence of it: footprints, flattened foliage."

"Let me e-mail him again before we start out. Maybe he didn't get the first one for some reason."

I sent yet another e-mail, letting him know we were at the cemetery and looking for him.

A quick check of the grounds and the van didn't turn up the monster hunter. Salinger grabbed three flashlights and a tool that could be used for prying from his car, and then we headed to the part of the cemetery where most of the crypts were. The first few we checked were locked up tight, but there was one in the second row that looked suspect.

"This one has footsteps all around it. Lots of footsteps," Zak said. "And the lock looks to have been broken as well."

Salinger used his weight to add leverage as he worked the heavy door open. The interior of the crypt was dark, the air stale. It was a family chamber, with rows of coffins on the side walls. There was a single coffin at the back as well.

"I don't see anything," I said as I shone my flashlight around.

"No. But someone's been in here," Zak replied. "Recently."

Salinger continued to shine his flashlight along the walls. He paused at each coffin to inspect it. I sure hoped he wasn't planning to open them.

"It's obvious the monster hunter isn't in here," I said as a chill ran down my spine. The shivers that had been absent inside the house had shown up here and brought friends. "If he was here we'd see him. Maybe we should just go."

"We'd only see him if he were out in the open," Zak corrected me.

"Maybe the local vampire didn't want anyone digging around in his business and Orson Spalding became victim number two," Salinger suggested.

I made a face. "You think he's in one of these coffins?"

Salinger opened the lid on the one at the back of the room. "I don't think so; I know so."

I don't know why I didn't follow my instinct to stay back. Almost against my will, I found myself inching forward. When I got close enough to see inside the coffin my stomach lurched. "Oh my God," I groaned.

"I know what you're thinking," Salinger said. "This town is crazy with people who are living out vampire fantasies, but I promise you, while this man obviously has been bitten, we're going to find the cause of death is most likely something injected into his bloodstream, like the venom that killed Irvine."

I didn't disagree, but the idea that a monster hunter had been killed by a monster seemed almost poetic to me. Still, while the injury to his neck indicated that someone had taken a big bite out of him, Salinger was probably right.

"If this man was in town to do a story on the vampire who killed Irvine, maybe he found something someone wanted to keep quiet," Zak said.

"It should be easy enough to find out where he was staying and get a look at his notes," Salinger said. "In the meantime, let's have a look at the inside of the van while we wait for the coroner to arrive for the body."

Chapter 12

The van was locked, but Salinger managed to pick the lock, allowing us to get a peek inside. The medical examiner had shown up and was with the body. Once he completed his initial inspection, he'd transport it to his office in Bryton Lake. He seemed to have things under control in the crypt, so our plan was first to search the van for any clues that might have been left behind, and then to head to whichever lodging the monster hunter had been staying.

"I wonder if he had a camera with him when he was attacked," Zak mused.

"I didn't see one," Salinger said.

"I didn't either, but we don't know where the attack actually occurred. There was plenty of blood in the coffin, but it also looked as if he put up a fight. I noticed scratches on his face and arms and his right hand was bloody, so I'm thinking he was attacked elsewhere, then taken to the coffin," Zak answered.

"Speaking of the coffin, what happened to the person who was originally buried there? I didn't see a skeleton laying around anywhere," I added.

"Good question." Salinger picked up a camera on top of a bin attached to the wall of the van. He turned it on and began scanning through the digital photos in the memory. "It looks like he's been spending quite a bit of time here. There are photos of men and women who look an awful lot like actual vampires walking around among the headstones after dark."

"So, if he'd already been out here filming the freak show that's descended on Ashton Falls, why was he out here today?" I asked. "We thought he might have wanted to get the lay of the land, but it appears he already had that covered."

Salinger looked at me. "When did you say this guy first showed up at the Zoo looking for you?"

I tried to remember. "I think it was Tuesday."

"And you sent off an e-mail to him right away?"

I nodded. "Within the hour of Jeremy telling me of his visit."

"Today's Friday. If he wanted to speak to you about the first vampire attack, I wonder why he hadn't responded to your e-mail before today."

"I have no idea. To be honest, with everything that's been going on, I forgot about it."

"Are we sure it was even Spalding who sent the e-mail today?" Zak asked.

Salinger rested his hand on the butt of his gun. "Now that you ask, I kind of doubt it. When exactly was the e-mail sent?"

I took out my phone and pulled up the e-mail. "Eleven twenty-one this morning."

"It's two thirty now. I'm going to speak to the ME now that he's had a chance to look at the body, but I'd be willing to bet we'll find that the time of death was a good twelve hours ago."

"So you think he was probably dead before the e-mail was sent," I said.

"If the victim didn't send it the killer must have." Zak's lips tightened. "Did you find the guy's phone?"

Salinger shook his head. "Not yet. But if the killer sent the e-mail and Spalding died at some point during the overnight hours, that explains a lot of things, such as why a man looking to film a vampire would be in a graveyard during the day, when he wasn't likely to run into any."

There was something about this scenario that wasn't lining up for me. Actually, there was *a lot* that wasn't, but I decided to tackle one problem at a time. "So, one of the vampires the monster hunter was here to film must have killed him when he was on location last night, then e-mailed me this morning. Why?" I furrowed my brow. "If Spalding was already dead why would the killer e-mail me at all? It's not like I'm part of the group. I doubt the killer even knows me."

"We've suspected from the beginning that there's someone out there playing with you," Zak reminded me. "He may or may not be linked to the group in town, but he definitely seems to want to get your attention."

I supposed Zak had a point. Maybe my being here to find this body as well was all part of a sick but very elaborate game.

"Is there anything in those photos that might help us figure this out?" I asked after a moment.

"I don't see a smoking gun, but I'll send all this equipment to the lab. If Spalding had a camera with him last night, which he probably did, that would be the one to find. Let's have a look around while we wait for the rest of the crime scene guys to show up. I'll have a chat with the ME so we can verify the time of death."

Zak and I went to Salinger's car to wait for him there. The sky was dark and the storm that everyone had been buzzing about seemed to be heading in our direction, but right now the breeze was soft and the temperature as close to perfect as an autumn afternoon could be. The thought of getting into the car and heading out for a leisurely drive around the lake had a lot of appeal. Not that a drive was in our future, but a person could fantasize.

"This is going to sound really odd," Zak said, "but for some reason, the memory of that picnic the whole family took last year during the fall color just popped into my head."

I smiled and wound my fingers through his. "I just thought something similar." I stopped and looked into the distance. "The day of the picnic started off sunny but ended up cloudy. I can still remember the brilliant yellow of the aspens along the river where we picnicked contrasting with the dark gray of the sky. I think the reason we're both thinking of that day is because of the aspens growing along the river on the mountain side of the road. Combined with the dark gray sky, the look is almost the same."

Zak looked toward the crypt, where Salinger was still talking with the ME. "Why don't we take a walk over to the river while Salinger's busy? He could be a while, and a walk beats sitting in the car."

"Okay. I'll text him to tell him what we're doing just in case he doesn't see us when he comes back."

The shallow river meandering around large rocks that were covered during the spring runoff was both serene and breathtakingly beautiful. The bright yellow leaves from the aspens were pooled in the nooks and crannies between the rocks. Zak took my hand and led me along the narrow dirt path that bordered the slowly moving water. The wind had picked up just a bit as the storm neared, though the moment was just about perfect.

"We should take the family for a picnic before the snow falls," I said as I rested my head on Zak's shoulder. "I know it's supposed to storm this weekend, but maybe the weekend following Halloween?"

"The leaves are already beginning to fall. If we get a significant storm this weekend it'll knock off the remaining ones. I'm afraid we may have missed our chance this year."

"Yeah." I sighed. "I guess you're right. Things have been so hectic this autumn."

"But we've had a lot of BBQs on the deck overlooking an aspen-lined lake. It isn't that we missed the fall color; it's just that we missed the fall drive and picnic. We'll make more of a point to fit it in next year."

"I feel like we need to make lists: things to do each fall, things to do each Christmas, things to do each summer. Do you know, we never once took the boat out for a full-moon cruise this past summer?"

"That's because Catherine is usually in bed before the moon rises, but I get your point. And making lists isn't a bad idea. I think we should turn back. Salinger should be wrapping things up by now."

"Yeah, okay." I paused to make the turn just as I noticed the rocks along the opposite shore. There was something on them that looked a lot like blood. "Look there." I pointed. "I think we might just have found the murder scene."

"I'll call Salinger," Zak said.

******

Not only had we found the murder scene, but a thorough search of the area netted us the camera Orson Spalding was most likely using to shoot footage of the nightly vampire walk when he was attacked. It was dark, and Spalding was shooting it from a distance. He was speaking softly, as if trying not to be noticed by those who'd come out for the role-playing event. It was spooky in a fun, Halloween sort of way. I'm not saying I'm going to trade in my mom jeans for black leather, red silk, and fangs, but if the two people who were dead were taken off the table, I could see how coming out and walking around in a dark cemetery in the middle of the night could provide a spark of terror that got long-atrophied brain cells firing.

Maybe the vampire role-playing thing was a bit over the top, but as I watched the video Spalding had shot, I could see how busy executives bored with their lives and needing a thrill might be in to it. That is, until we came to the last scene Spalding would ever shoot.

"What are you doing here?" Spalding's voice could be heard in the background, but the camera remained on the men and women in the cemetery.

"This is my gig. I warned you to pack up and leave," an unidentified voice said.

"You're veering into my territory now, and I'm not going to let some two-bit wannabe tell me what I can and can't do."

There was a snarl I assumed came from the second man. "In this last moment of your life I want you to remember it was your choice to ignore my warnings. Such a shame really, but I suppose there's only room for one of us."

"What are you doing? Are you crazy?"

After that the camera must have fallen to the ground. All that could be seen through the lens was the dark sky, but the sounds of a struggle could be heard in the background. Eventually, the struggle ceased and there was silence. Someone picked up the camera and turned it off.

"Okay, that was disturbing," I said to Zak.

"Right there with you. It sounds like the man who killed Spalding was a rival of some sort."

"Rival what?" I asked. "Rival monster hunter, rival filmmaker, rival vampire, assuming Spalding participated in the role-playing and didn't just film it."

"I wish I knew." Zak scratched his chin. "Did the voice of the other man sound kind of familiar to you?"

I frowned. "Now that you mention it, his voice did seem similar, although for the life of me, I can't place it. Do you think the killer is someone local? Maybe someone we don't know well but run in to and chat with, like one of the checkers at the grocery store or someone who works in a local restaurant?"

"Maybe." Zak glanced at the camera again. "I can't believe Orson Spalding's murder was recorded but there isn't a single video image of the killer."

"There might be fingerprints on the camera. We need to get this to Salinger right away."

I glanced around the area one last time before we headed back to Salinger's car. It seemed if Spalding was murdered while filming the late-night vampire fest someone would have overheard the scuffle. Sure, Spalding was hiding across the road from the cemetery, I assumed, so he could make the recording without being seen, but the sound of a man being brutally murdered would have carried the fifty yards or so between where Spalding was hiding and the cemetery. Why hadn't anyone intervened?

"Don't you think it's odd that no one called in Spalding's murder?" I asked Zak. "From that footage, it appears as if he was killed less than a football field away from a cemetery where at least a dozen men and women were hanging around playing dress-up."

"It does seem as if the group in the cemetery would have overheard what was going on. Maybe it isn't uncommon for people to be murdered during these things."

I wrinkled my nose. "I didn't pick up a ritual sacrifice vibe from what was going on in the video. Spalding's death was personal. Hopefully, Salinger will be able to pull some prints, or maybe the guys at the lab can use voice recognition software to find out who the other man on the tape is."

"For voice recognition to work you have to have something to compare it to. But you're right; that voice sounded familiar. Maybe if the killer is a local Salinger will recognize his voice."

Salinger was walking toward the car as we came closer. "What do you have there?" he asked.

"We found the murder scene and the video camera Spalding was using to film the vampire walk when he was attacked."

Salinger raised a brow. "His murder was caught on film? Who did it?"

"We don't know," I admitted. "The camera is trained on the sky the whole time, but the audio was on. Maybe the guys at the lab can find something concrete that points to the killer. It sounds like the guy who killed Spalding did so because he considered the vampire festivities in Ashton Falls to be his gig and Spalding was worming in on his territory."

Salinger stood holding the camera with the oddest expression on his face. "When you say Spalding was killed for worming into the killer's territory it almost makes it seem as if the first victim, Edgar Irvine, was killed to create the hype that got the vampires to come to Ashton Falls in the first place."

"It does seem that way," Zak agreed. "Especially when it looks as though the tabloid might have been tipped off before the murder even happened."

"If the motive for Irvine's murder was to bring a bunch of vampire wannabees to Ashton Falls, why Irvine and why involve me?" I asked. "The killer had to lure Irvine here from Hollywood, and that seems intentional and specific."

"Maybe the killer had a reason to involve both of you and a reason to want a bunch of vampire types to gather," Salinger said.

"Which would mean there was a link between me and Irvine," I said. "I swear I'd never seen him before and I promise I don't have a creature-of-the-night fetish, so how is it possible I'm linked to either Irvine or the killer?"

"You don't have to be linked to each other; you only both have to be linked to the killer," Zak said. "We both thought we recognized the voice of the man who killed Spalding, which means he might be local, which would explain how he knows you and why he chose Ashton Falls as the location of his vampire fest. What we need to figure out is who it is and how he knew Irvine. If we go back to the whole why-that-snake thought, I'd say Irvine's assistant, Becka, is probably the link between the killer and Irvine."

"So we need to dig into Becka's life and see who pops," I said. I looked at Salinger. "Are you ready to go, or should I call someone to come pick us up?"

"I can drop you off at home. I want to get this camera to the lab right away. Maybe the killer left a print behind. After that I'm going to Spalding's hotel room. Maybe there are notes or photos there that will help us figure this out."

After Salinger took us to the house, Zak and I greeted everyone, then sequestered ourselves in the computer room to dig around in Becka Watson's life. It seemed she might be the key to everything.

Chapter 13

An hour into his search, Zak said, "Rebecca Watson was born to Mavis and Oliver Watson in a small town in Kansas twenty-five years ago. She was an only child and her mother died of pneumonia when she was twelve. Four months later, her father died of a heart attack. The Watsons didn't have family who were willing or able to take Rebecca on a full-time basis, so she went into foster care, where she began to be called Becka. Becka was a bright girl who did well in school. After high school she was awarded a college scholarship that allowed her to obtain a degree in history. She took a couple of years off after obtaining her bachelor's degree before deciding to return to school to engage in graduate work. It was while she was attending graduate school that she met Edgar Irvine, who paid her generously to help him with his research."

"Interesting, but hardly anything relevant to this case," I said.

"Perhaps. But according to Carl Poland, Becka had a brother who was part of the same role-playing group Irvine belonged to. He thought his name was Matt or Mitch or something."

"That's right," I acknowledged. "But it doesn't sound as if she had a brother after all."

"Unless he was a foster brother."

"You said one of Irvine's ex-assistants thought the brother's name was Mason. Were you able to find a Mason Watson?"

"I didn't have a chance to look into that yet, but if the man people have been referring to is a foster brother, his last name won't be Watson anyway."

"It's going to be hard to track him down without a last name, and we still aren't even sure about the first name."

Zak let out a long, slow sigh. "I'll dig around for anyone in Becka's contacts with a first name beginning with M. Once I have a list I'll try to narrow it down to one individual. The film we found today makes it seem as if the person who killed Orson Spalding was some sort of a competitor, not the enraged brother of a woman who died due to the carelessness of the first victim, so I'm not sure our theory that Becka's brother might be the killer is holding up anyway, unless there are two killers, which there might be. Still, it can't hurt to identify Becka's brother if she had one. If he isn't the killer maybe he knows who might have wanted Irvine dead."

"So you think the two deaths might be unrelated?" I asked.

Zak shrugged. "I wouldn't say unrelated, but I am entertaining the possibility of two killers. Irvine seemed to have been lured here. That speaks to me of a specific intention and motivation. From the video, it almost sounded like Spalding was killed because he was in the way. Of course, there are a lot of similarities between the two men as well. The first victim was a screenwriter focusing on paranormal activity who was also in to role-playing games. The second was linked to both television and the paranormal, and he may have been in to the role-playing games he filmed. The vampires overrunning Ashton Falls were lured here by an article in a tabloid that appears to have been written before the victim discussed in the article was even dead. It seems the killer or someone associated with him had to have written it. From the limited percentage of the population I assume is in to the vampire role-playing thing, I might conclude the two deaths were linked. However, I'm not sure if and how Becka's death fits into the overall scenario, except for the fact that the venom used to kill the first victim was very specific."

I got up and began to pace. "We must be missing a piece to the puzzle. An important piece that allows everything to fit. At this point I agree with you: the two deaths seem to be related in some aspects but not in others."

"I suppose all we can do right now is keep working on it. Eventually, things will come together."

"Maybe. I hope so. I'd like to get my life back." I glanced at the clock. "I'm going to check with everyone, figure out what we'll do for dinner. You keep at it."

Mom, Ellie, and Alex were sitting at the dining table sipping tea while they discussed how the rain that had started up within the past thirty minutes was going to affect Haunted Hamlet. If the rain persisted the outdoor activities would most likely be a total bust. Scooter was in the family room with Tucker, whose aunt had dropped him off for the weekend after school. When I'd suggested Tucker spend the night on Saturday I hadn't meant he should spend the entire weekend with us, but Scooter was bored being cooped up in the house, so having a friend with him would help.

I made a cup of tea and sat down at the table with the others. "Are Catherine and Eli still napping?" I asked.

"They are, although I was planning to get them up in the next twenty minutes," Ellie answered. "How goes the investigation?"

"We're making progress, but it's slow going. I needed a break, and we need to talk about dinner. Are you both planning to stay?" I asked Mom and Ellie.

"Ava and her family are coming to our place for dinner tonight, so your dad is picking up me and Harper when he closes the store," Mom said.

"But you're coming back tomorrow to help me with my makeup for the dance, right?" Alex asked.

Mom smiled. "I wouldn't miss it for the world."

I glanced at Ellie. "How about you guys?"

"I need to check with Levi, but I'm sure he'll be up for hanging out," Ellie said. "We don't have any plans. The rain doesn't look like it's going to let up, so eating outdoors is off. Maybe I'll make some soup. I don't have time for bean or pea, but maybe broccoli cheese or hearty man stew."

"Soup sounds perfect," I agreed. "I'm not sure if we have everything you'll need, though."

Ellie stood up. "I'll take a look. I can have Levi run by the store on his way over. I'm sure football practice will be cut short with the rain."

"I'll go upstairs and rouse the babies," I offered. "I'll change them and bring them down. I feel like I've barely even seen Catherine these past few days."

I decided to get Eli up first. He was a bit more agreeable about being woken before he was ready. When I arrived in the room in which Eli had a crib I found him sitting up, playing with a truck he'd managed to maneuver off the nearby dresser.

"Hey, big guy. Look at you, playing all nice and quiet."

Eli stood up and reached out his arms, and I picked him up and snuggled him close. I used my free hand to swipe his longish brown hair from his eyes.

"Doggy," Eli said, pointing.

I turned around to see Charlie had followed me into the room. "Yes. Let's get you changed and you can play with him while I rouse Catherine."

"Ball," Eli said after I laid him on the changing table.

I picked up the small rubber football he often played with. "Are you going to be a football player like your daddy?"

"Dada," Eli said before putting the end of the ball in his mouth.

When Eli was dry and refreshed I picked him up and headed to the nursery. I set Eli and his football on the blanket I had put on the floor, then nodded at Charlie that it was okay to play with Eli before heading over to the crib, where my little princess was still sleeping.

"Time to wake up, sunshine," I said as I gently rubbed Catherine's back.

She opened one eye, which must have been enough for her to see Eli playing with Charlie because she sat right up and reached her arms to me. As I'd done with Eli, I gave her something to hold while I changed her, then I picked up both babies, one in each arm, and went down the stairs with Charlie following behind us.

"There's my guy," Ellie said as Eli reached for her.

Catherine saw Harper and reached for her, so I set her on the floor with her auntie.

"Harper is having so much fun with the babies," Mom said. "It makes me feel bad she doesn't have a sibling."

"Uh, what about me?" I waved my hand.

Mom laughed. "Of course, dear. I would never forget you. But while you're Harper's sister, you're more of an aunt in terms of age and relationship. What I was trying to say in an extremely clumsy way was that I was sorry it didn't work out for Harper to have a sibling close to her own age."

"I knew what you meant," I said. "I was just giving you a hard time. And I agree, a sibling would have been nice. I always wanted one, but I had Ellie and Levi, and it was almost like having a sister and brother. Harper has Eli and Catherine, and her BFF, Morgan," I added, referring to Jeremy's daughter, who was born within days of her.

"That's true. Harper's lucky to have so many awesome friends in her life."

I looked at Ellie. "Can I help?"

"Zak came in looking for coffee a few minutes ago," Ellie answered as she stirred a pot of something that smelled wonderful. "He told me to send you into the computer room when you came down. It seems he might have news."

I glanced at Catherine. She seemed happy playing with Eli, Harper, and Charlie, but I felt bad about leaving her again. The best thing I could do for everyone's piece of mind, I thought, was to get this mystery solved, so I gave her a kiss, then headed to the office.

"Good, you're here," Zak said.

"What's up? Did you find something?"

"Becka had a foster brother named Mason Kellerman. The two of them lived in the same house for over a year when they were teens. They both had a problem fitting in with the other kids but seemed to get along with each other. They became close and stayed in touch after they both moved on. After he turned eighteen, Mason moved around a lot. In fact, I can't find evidence of him settling down much at all. There are several gaps in his history, the most recent covering an eight-year period. It appears he might have lived under an alias at times, though he might have been out of the country during those gaps. Currently, he's in LA. As far as I can tell, he's had the same address for about three years. Like the monster hunter, he works in film. Low-budget paranormal stuff."

My eyes got big. "So, you found the connection. Mason Kellerman was linked to the first victim, who was responsible for his foster sister's death, and the second victim via his field, which seems to have made them competitors."

Zak nodded. "And we've also been told he belonged to the same role-playing group Irvine did. He might even be in Ashton Falls right now. I talked to Salinger. He's trying to track him down through lodging records. There's still one huge unanswered question, though. We have no idea what any of this has to do with you, yet you seem to be involved."

"Yeah." I sighed. There was still that small, pesky fact.

Chapter 14

Saturday, October 27

Zak and I decided to take the family to the Haunted Hamlet for a few hours on Saturday morning. It was still cool and drizzly, but the rain was far from steady, and if we dressed warm and pulled rain slickers on top, we'd be fine. Levi and Ellie came with us, as did Nona, so it was a large group that piled into vans and headed to the center of town.

"It's nice the rain has stopped for the time being," Nona said as we drove toward the park where the food court and kiddie carnival had been set up.

"Me and Tucker want to go to the haunted house," Scooter said.

"We will after we eat. I'll wait with the babies while the rest of you go in," I offered.

"I'll wait with you," Ellie offered, rubbing her large stomach. "I don't think the stress of having people jump out at me would be the best thing for baby Denton. In fact," Ellie looked at me, "if you want to go in I can sit with Eli and Catherine."

"Are we going to eat at the food court?" Alex asked. "If we are we might want to do that first. There are only a limited number of tables under the tent and if we don't grab one, we'll be eating outside where the tables are wet from the rain."

"I could eat," I said. "Ellie and I will grab a table large enough for all of us. You all can go and get the food."

"What do you want?" Zak asked me.

"A BBQ pork sandwich with potato salad."

The others went to the food counter while Ellie and I settled at a covered table large enough for ten. Eli and Catherine were snuggled into a double-wide stroller and seemed content for the time being, so we'd left them there at least until the food arrived.

"It seems there's a pretty good turnout despite the rain," Ellie said as we scanned the crowd.

"I figured the line for the haunted house would be crazy because it's an indoor event, but I'm surprised to see so many people in the park. Of course, Haunted Hamlet is a tradition for a lot of people. It makes sense we wouldn't be the only ones who braved the elements to come. I wonder how the zombie run went this morning. It was raining pretty steadily then."

"I bet there was a good turnout. The zombie runners get pretty muddy even when there's no rain."

I waved to Tawny Upton, who was on her way to the food line with her children. Tawny had started a daycare center so she could have her children at work with her when they were young. By this point they were all in public school, but her place was doing as well as it ever had.

"I heard Tawny and that guy she's been seeing are getting really serious," Ellie commented. "There's even talk of an engagement."

I thought about the man. He was good-looking for sure, and he seemed to have an easygoing way about him, but I found something off about him. "Did he ever get a job?"

"Tawny said he hoped to open a personal security business, or maybe it was surveillance; I'm not sure. It might even have been something like private investigation. I think I remember hearing he was taking some class."

"Seems intentionally vague. Almost like he has no intention of becoming gainfully employed but talks a lot about a new venture to make it seem as if he's working on it."

"Yeah. He's been mooching off Tawny for at least six months. If I were her, I'd put a brake on things until he started bringing in some income. Although she's really in to him, and from what I hear, he's great with her kids."

I glanced at Tawny again as she made her way through the long line. The concept of a PI or a PI wannabe was giving me an idea about my stalker. Zak and I had concluded that the odds that the person who'd taken all the photos of me and one who'd killed the two men being the same person were fifty-fifty at best. "I need to ask Tawny a question about the class her boyfriend is taking. Can you keep an eye on Catherine for a minute? Zak and the others are almost to the front of the line, so they should be here in just a few minutes."

"No problem. But hurry. You won't want your food to get cold."

I jogged across the lawn to Tawny and her kids, halfway to the food.

"Hey, Zoe. Are you having fun so far?"

"I am." I glanced at Zak, who was paying for the food. "I need to get back, but I had a question about the class I heard your boyfriend is taking. Is it true he wants to get into surveillance?"

"Jason wants to open a business that combines it and investigation with private security. What he's taking isn't so much a class as a competition. He's hoping to win and use the prize money to open his company."

"Tell me about this competition."

Tawny motioned for her kids to move up in the line. "I don't know all the details, but apparently, some big security firm is sponsoring it. Each contestant is assigned a subject they follow for a month. They're supposed to take photos of a subject, then write up a report on the person they've been surveilling. There are specific questions to answer about the person's routine, that sort of thing."

"So, Jason is stalking someone to compete for a cash prize."

Tawny shrugged. "I guess it could be considered invasive to the person being observed, but PIs do it all the time. I think it's pretty harmless."

Harmless wasn't the word I'd use, given the fact that someone had been stalking me and I knew how violated it made me feel. "Any idea who your boyfriend's subject is?"

Tawny shook her head. "He didn't tell me. He hasn't told anyone. I don't think he's supposed to.

The whole thing is very hush-hush, just the way it would be for a real private investigator."

I had a feeling I knew exactly who he'd been assigned to watch. I'd need to confirm it, but Tawny's boyfriend was physically similar to the man whose reflection we'd picked out in the semi, so I was sure my suspicion would bear out.

I returned to the table, where Zak and the others were chowing down on their lunch. I sat down next to him and leaned in close. "I think I know who my stalker is."

Zak paused with his burger halfway to his mouth. "Who?"

"Tawny's boyfriend. His name is Jason, and he's supposedly in some contest to win a cash prize by surveilling someone for a month."

Zak frowned. "That doesn't sound kosher to me."

"It sounds wrong to me too. I'm going to call Salinger after we finish eating and run the idea past him."

******

When I'd called Salinger he'd been tied up, so we set up a meeting for two o'clock. That worked out fine for me because it gave Zak and Levi time to take Nona and the kids through the haunted house while Ellie and I took the babies to see the rubber duck race that ran from the river near the park to the lake where it emptied out. Prior to having a baby, the race had never interested me, but now I found it to be a lot more fun than I'd anticipated. Not that either Eli or Catherine's ducky came even close to winning, but it was fun to cheer the ducks along as they made their short journey.

After the haunted house crowd had returned we all headed home. Levi and Ellie took both babies to their place for their naps, while Nona and the older kids were dropped off at our house. My mom was due to come by at four to help Alex with her makeup, but I figured we'd be back well before then.

At the sheriff's office, Salinger was sitting behind his desk working on a file. He set it aside when we walked in. "So, you think you found your stalker?" he asked.

I explained about Jason and the contest he was participating in. Salinger agreed that on the surface it sounded as if he could be our guy, so he radioed one of the deputies who were in Ashton Falls helping out for the weekend and asked him to bring Jason in for questioning. While we were waiting for him to arrive, we looked through the photos one more time. I'd gone through the ones Salinger had made copies of and left for me, but we realized that if Jason didn't 'fess up to following me, a photo with his reflection might just provide the incentive he'd need to come clean.

"The photos we found in the barn seem pretty harmless," I said. "Most are of me going about my daily business. Dropping Scooter off at school, taking the dogs for a walk, shopping, spending time at the Zoo. But there's this one that sends little shivers down my spine."

I handed it to Zak.

He frowned.

"What is it?" Salinger asked.

Zak passed the photo to Salinger. "I don't remember seeing this one the first time I went through the box."

"Because it wasn't in the box. At least not initially," I said.

Salinger furrowed his brow. "What do you mean, it wasn't in the box? Of course it was. It has to have been."

I shook my head. "The photo is of Zak and me while we walked along the river, waiting for you to speak to the medical examiner. It was taken a few minutes before we stumbled across the crime scene." I pointed at the photo. "We were talking about a trip we once took with a similar setting to this river walk."

"That was yesterday," Salinger said.

"Exactly. I found the box of photos in the barn on Wednesday."

"That's impossible," Salinger huffed. "This box has been in my office since I put it here the day you discovered it."

I looked at the photo again. It had definitely been taken yesterday. "Maybe someone slipped in and added the photo to the box."

"Why would anyone do that?" Salinger asked.

"Why would anyone do anything that's happened this past week? We're obviously dealing with a psycho."

"Then let me change my question," Salinger said. "How would someone slip in and add the photo to the box? The front door to this building is locked any time I don't have a receptionist in front."

"Does she lock the door every time she takes a break to use the ladies' room?" I wondered.

Salinger frowned. "I don't know for certain, but probably not."

The room fell into silence until Salinger's phone buzzed, letting him know Jason was here. The sheriff asked that he be taken to the conference room that doubled as an interrogation room. Salinger wanted to speak to him alone, but he was fine with Zak and me watching through the two-way glass.

"Why am I here?" the very angry man demanded the minute Salinger walked through the door.

Salinger tossed a handful of photos onto the table. "Do you recognize these?"

He paled. "I wondered what happened to those."

"So they are yours?" Salinger asked.

He nodded.

"I'm going to need a verbal reply," Salinger demanded.

"Yes. I took the photos. For a contest. It's all perfectly innocent."

Salinger sat down on a hard plastic chair across from Jason. "Why don't you start at the beginning and tell me exactly why it is you've been following Mrs. Zimmerman around for the past few weeks snapping photos of her?"

He ran a hand through his dark hair. "Am I in some sort of trouble?"

"You're most definitely in some sort of trouble. How much trouble will depend on how cooperative you are."

He nodded, then glanced at the two-way mirror, frowned, and began to speak. "Like I said, I took the photos as part of a contest."

Salinger took out a notepad and pen. "I'll need the name of the contest, the name of your contact person, and the names of the other contestants if you know them."

"I don't know any of that."

I thought he was about to cry.

Salinger clicked open his pen and closed it. "Okay. Let's start with how you found out about the contest."

Jason folded his hands, opened them again, and then ran them nervously over his pant legs. "I received an e-mail about a month ago, saying there was going to be one lucky winner who'd get ten thousand dollars. I needed ten thousand dollars, so I responded. I was sent a list of instructions and the name of my subject."

"Let's back up a bit," Salinger said. "You said you were sent an e-mail. Who sent it?"

"A company called Surveillance Masters."

"Was the e-mail personalized to you?" Salinger asked.

Jason nodded.

"I'll need a verbal reply," Salinger reminded him.

He bowed his head. "Oh, sorry. Yes, the e-mail was personalized to me."

Salinger jotted down a note. "And how do you think this company got your name?"

"I assume it was because of the class I signed up for."

Salinger lifted a brow. "Class?"

"I signed up for a class that teaches you how to do surveillance, for folks wanting to go into private investigation and related fields. When I got the e-mail I just assumed I was invited to enter the competition because I'd shown interest in the field by signing up for the class."

Jason was probably right about that.

Salinger flipped his notepad to a clean sheet. "So you responded to the e-mail and then what?"

"Then I got a return e-mail with the rules. I was to follow Mrs. Zimmerman for a month, remaining undetected as I did so. I was to take photos of her, and from those photos I was supposed to come to some conclusions."

"What sort of conclusions?" Salinger asked.

"Just stuff like whether she was stepping out on her husband."

Zak glanced at me with a raised brow. I smiled and shook my head. Zak wound the fingers of his left hand through my right and gave it a gentle squeeze.

Jason continued. "There were a whole list of questions I was supposed to answer, like whether there were routines she kept on certain days of the week or certain times of the day. I knew she went to the events committee every Wednesday because my girlfriend did too, and I knew she picked up her son from school on most days at three fifteen because I sometimes picked up my girlfriend's kids at the same time. I found out she walks her dogs every day at around four thirty or five, and she almost always turns to the left down the beach after leaving her house. Stuff like that. The more detailed my observations, the more points I'd receive."

"Were you supposed to report on things other than her routine?" Salinger asked.

"I was to make a list of the people she spent the most time with and make notes about personal routines, such as exercise classes she might be taking and things like that."

"Why did you hide the photos in the barn at Henderson House?"

"I didn't. They were in my apartment until a few days ago. I got an e-mail that my challenge was complete on Monday of this week. I was also notified that someone from the contest had stopped by to pick up the photos. I thought that was odd because I keep my place locked when I go out, but I didn't find anything tampered with or missing, so I let it go."

Which meant someone else had put the photos in the barn. How many people were involved in this thing anyway? I found myself becoming increasingly frustrated.

"Do you have the e-mails you were sent and the list of items to provide in your surveillance?" Salinger asked.

"Yes."

"I'll need you to deliver everything to me, including all the e-mails you've received from Surveillance Masters."

Jason nodded vigorously. "I'll give you everything. I don't want to go to jail."

Salinger didn't respond to that. Instead, he tossed another photo in front of Jason. "Tell me about this one."

Jason picked it up. He looked at it with a frown, then said, "I didn't take this photo."

"Are you sure?" Salinger asked. "Remember, I'm expecting your full cooperation."

Jason looked up at Salinger. "I'm sure. If I'd taken it I'd tell you, but I didn't." He narrowed his gaze. "I don't even know where this is."

I wasn't surprised Jason hadn't taken the photo by the river. That one, I was certain, had been taken by the killer.

Chapter 15

Salinger questioned Jason for another thirty minutes before allowing him to leave. I was happy we'd identified my stalker, but doing so hadn't brought us any closer to identifying the killer. By the time we got home my mom was there. Zak walked over to Levi and Ellie's to pick up Catherine while I went upstairs to join the others.

"How'd it go?" Mom asked.

"Jason admitted to being the one to take the photos of me. I'm happy to know it was just some guy with bad judgment and a desire to win ten grand and not a psycho killer following me these past few weeks, but his confession didn't bring us at all closer to finding out who killed the two murder victims."

"Seems like it might be Salinger's job to figure that out," Mom said as she teased Alex's hair.

"Maybe, but I still feel I've been intentionally linked to the death of both men, so I don't think I'll be able to relax completely until the killer is caught."

I sat down on the edge of Alex's bed. She was sitting at her vanity while Mom did her magic with her makeup. "Having said that, I've done what I can for today and am very excited to see Alex's transformation." I stopped talking long enough to take a look at the makeup Mom was applying. It seemed to feature a lot of really dark eye makeup. "I thought you were going as Marie Curie."

"I was, but Diego and I changed our minds at the last minute. I'm going as Cleopatra and he's Marc Antony."

Okay, that had me frowning. Most of the Cleopatra outfits I'd seen over the years featured a very skimpy outfit with a bare midriff. Zak would blow his lid.

"Is it okay if I see your costume?" I asked.

"Sure," Alex said. "It's hanging on the back of the closet door. I borrowed it from my friend Evie, who was Cleopatra last year."

I let out a sigh of relief when I saw that the dress, while sleeveless, was long enough to touch the floor. The headdress that went with it was really outstanding. Alex, with her long dark hair, was going to make a beautiful Cleopatra. Now I just hoped Diego's Marc Antony costume was equally modest.

Mom sat back and admired her handiwork. "I wish I had my liquid eyeliner. I'd be able to accomplish the cat's-eye effect a lot more easily." She looked at me. "I don't suppose you have any?"

I laughed. "Me? No, I don't think so. I can run out and get some, though."

"Don't bother. I can make do with what I have."

I placed my hand on my heart as I looked at Alex. "You look so grown-up."

"That," Alex smiled, "is exactly what I was going for."

"Zoe," I heard Ellie call from somewhere down the hallway.

I stuck my head out the door. "I'm in Alex's room. Is something wrong?"

"I let the dogs out into the yard for a few minutes and when I called them back everyone came running except Charlie."

"That's odd. I'll go out to see if I can find him. Is Zak back with Catherine yet?"

"I haven't seen him."

I headed to the back door. It wasn't at all like Charlie to wander off. The other dogs became distracted from time to time, but Charlie always stayed close to the house when he was let out without a human.

"Charlie," I called.

I paused, but there was no reply. I headed toward the beach. As I passed Mr. and Mrs. Frankenstein, which Zak and Scooter had set up earlier in the week, I felt a chill run down my spine. I stopped to look at the mechanical figures, which had been repaired but once had been damaged due to my anger and negligence. I continued on down the beach, hugging the waterline. I didn't see anyone, but I had the feeling I was being watched.

"Charlie," I called again.

It was then I heard a single sharp bark.

"Charlie, where are you?"

The single bark turned to a series of barks. It sounded like he was somewhere down the beach, so I took off at a jog in that direction. The barking grew more insistent and I became increasingly worried.

The only way Charlie wouldn't come was if he was hurt and unable to do so. I ran faster. About a quarter mile down the beach from the house I found him tied to a tree.

"Charlie." I fell to my knees and hugged my little pal. I was about to untie him when I heard a voice behind me.

"Leave him tied up or I'll have to kill him."

I turned and looked at the man behind me. "I should have known it was you."

He looked genuinely hurt. "I'm offended you didn't figure it out long before this. I did, after all, go to quite a lot of trouble."

"What do you want?"

"What I want is for you to come with me. I have something to show you."

"I'm not going anywhere with you," I said with a bravado I wasn't quite feeling, given the fact that he had a gun on me.

Joel Ringer sneered. "You can come along all peaceful-like, or I can put a bullet in your mutt's head. Your choice."

Damn. The psycho had me and he knew it. I'd never risk Charlie's life. "What do you want to show me?"

"I have a boat nearby. We'll need to take a little trip. Come along nicely and both you and the dog will live. Fight me and you'll both die."

I wanted to attack him with the full force of my five-foot-nothing rage, but I'd never be able to live with myself if something happened to Charlie, so I turned and followed Joel meekly down the beach.

"You know this infatuation you seem to have with me has got to stop," I said after we'd arrived at the boat and set off across the lake. "Killing two men just to impress me really is way over the top," I taunted him, even though the little voice in my head was screaming at me to just shut up.

"As fond as I am of you, I'm afraid I didn't do that."

"You didn't kill Edgar Irvine and Orson Spalding?"

Joel chuckled. "Oh, I killed them, but if I impressed you with my technique it was simply a side benefit of what I was going to do anyway."

I turned slightly so I was facing him. "Okay, so why did you kill Irvine and Spalding?" I probably should have been using this time to try to escape, but Joel had a gun and we were in the middle of a large lake. All I really could do was wait to see how things played out.

"Irvine killed my sister."

I raised a brow. "So you're Mason Kellerman?"

Joel nodded. "Mason Kellerman was my first name. I've gone by many others in my life. When you knew me, I was Joel Ringer. Before that I was Elon Midnight for a time."

"I'm sorry."

Joel looked at me with an expression of surprise. "You're sorry?"

"About your sister. I don't know everything that happened to her, but I know enough to realize her death probably could have been avoided. I know how hard it is to lose someone you love. Someone who helped you to make sense of a life that doesn't always make sense. I'm not saying I approve of you killing Irvine, but I guess I understand the rage behind such an action."

Joel's face softened. "Thank you."

"I am curious, though, why you did things the way you did. The venom from an African black mamba must have been pricey. Why go to all the bother? Why not use the venom of a rattler?"

Joel scowled. "A rattler would never do. You know me well enough to realize how important it is to have just the right prop to bring a level of authenticity to something."

Joel was the king of the props. During his time in Ashton Falls, he'd presented some pretty spectacular haunted houses. If a ghost hunter hadn't come to town and accidentally stumbled onto Joel's big secret, he might still be living here, putting on shows the way no one else ever could.

"Besides," Joel continued, "the venom didn't cost me a thing. I used some of the money I stole from Edgar."

"You stole money from Edgar Irvine to buy the venom you used to kill him?"

Joel grinned. "Poetic, don't you think?"

I wasn't sure *poetic* was the word I'd use, but I guess there was a certain artistry to what he'd done. "Let me be sure I understand this. You found out Irvine was responsible for your sister's death. You wanted to take vengeance on him, so you stole money from him that you used to procure venom from the same type of snake that killed her. You developed a device to deliver the venom to his bloodstream through his neck, which made it look like a vampire bite— which, by the way, was kind of cool in a deranged kind of way. I understand you're in to role-playing, so making it look like a vampire attack fit too. The thing that doesn't make sense is why Ashton Falls and why me?"

"Because, love, you're the one who got away. You not only foiled my plan but you sent me into hiding for four years. My plan now had to include a resolution to the scenario in which tiny Zoe Donovan meets a monster and comes out the winner."

"I'm guessing you're the monster in this scenario."

Joel just grinned.

I took a breath and blew it out slowly. I might be minutes from my untimely death, but at least I had most of my answers. Joel had gone to a lot of trouble to pull this together. He really was the master. He'd managed to whet Irvine's appetite to the point that he made the trip to Ashton Falls. He bought rare snake venom with money he stole from the victim and he used the death of the man who killed his sister to get a bunch of other vampire types to make the trip to Ashton Falls too, presumably so he could film the movie he seemed to have been chasing his entire life.

"So the news article in the tabloid was a ploy to get vampires to show. I'm assuming you were filming them?"

"You assume correctly."

"But monster hunter Orson Spalding showed up and tried to cash in on all your hard work, so you had to kill him as well."

Joel made a hard left that sent me to the floor of the speeding craft. "Hey," I yelled. "Was that necessary?"

Joel laughed. "Necessary, no. Fun, absolutely."

He began to slow the boat. When he stopped at a point I figured was smack-dab in the middle of the lake, I began to panic. It had to be at least five miles to the nearest land. Surely he wasn't going to dump me overboard. But a five-mile swim presented a chance. A bullet to the head, not so much.

"Maybe now would be a good time for you to tell me why you brought me on this lovely journey."

"I'm afraid our time together has come to an end. I really thought killing Irvine and finally making my movie would somehow make me feel better, but it didn't. In fact, all I feel is empty. Still, I'll admit that you, Zoe Donovan, have added a certain level of spice to my life. Sure, you messed things up for me four years ago, but looking back, I think I'd been searching for a worthy adversary my entire life. It's been a privilege to know you."

"A privilege to know me?" I said in a voice that sounded high and squeaky. "Are you going to kill me?"

"Kill you? Do you doubt my word? I told you that if you came peacefully your life as well as the life of your little dog would be spared."

I narrowed my gaze and dared to look Joel in the eye. "You did say that. But your speech sounded a bit like a last farewell."

Joel's smile faded. "Alas, it was a last farewell. There comes a time when the final curtain must come down, and I'm afraid that for me, this is that time. Here's hoping we meet in the next life."

I'm not sure exactly what happened next. Joel dove into the water, which left me stunned and confused. I held my breath and waited for him to surface, but he never did. It took me several seconds at least for it to sink in that Joel had most likely dove straight down beyond the point where returning to the surface was a possibility. When the reality of the situation sank in, I used my cell phone to call Salinger. Then I kicked off my shoes and dove into the water to see if I could find the madman who I was pretty sure had just committed suicide.

Chapter 16

Wednesday October 31

Getting over the horror of Joel Ringer's death was a lot more difficult for me than I'd anticipated. I'd never know for certain why he'd made the choices he had, but I suspected Becka had been his ground in this crazy world, and once she was gone, his connection to it was gone as well. The dive team never did find Joel's body, but I hadn't seen him surface, and even if he had, there was little chance he could swim all the way to the nearest land mass. I supposed there were people who could swim that far, though, so maybe…?

On a more positive note, Jeremy had managed to track down the owner of our mama stray, who was delighted to find her after almost giving up on hope of doing so. The dog had been missing for over a month and the owner hadn't known the dog was pregnant when she disappeared from her yard. She was delighted to take both the mama and her babies home with her.

And on an even better note, the Zoe Donovan-Zimmerman Halloween Spooktacular was underway, and everything had turned out perfectly.

"Good turnout," Hazel said when she joined Ellie and me in the kitchen, where we were putting finger foods on trays.

"It seems like everyone is here, although I haven't seen Grandpa."

"He's here," Hazel assured me. "The last I saw, he was sitting at the pool bar with your dad and Ethan. Can I help?"

"We're just transferring the food from the cookie sheets and refrigerator containers onto serving trays," I said. "The trays are stacked on the table. Just grab a cookie sheet or storage container and start moving."

Hazel took a cookie sheet with hot wontons from the countertop and began making the transfer. "I spoke to your mother. She said she's going to join the events committee."

I nodded. "She spoke to Hillary yesterday. I think she'll do a great job. She has more experience planning things than anyone in town and she'll fill the void, now that Ellie and I are thinking about taking a step back."

"She seems to be willing to jump in with both feet. I hear she might even take on Hometown Christmas as the new chair, now that Tawny backed out."

"Tawny backed out?" I asked. I hadn't heard that.

"She broke up with her boyfriend because of the stalking fiasco. She's pretty down in the dumps, and while I do feel bad for her, I think it's for the best.

She needs a nice stable man in her life. One who'll be a true partner and help her raise her kids. Even before we found out he was your stalker, it never seemed he was going to pull his weight as part of a team."

I felt bad for Tawny, who seemed to have gone from one failed relationship to another, but Hazel wasn't wrong. I too hoped she'd find someone worthy of her affection.

After I finished off the tray I was working on I stood back to admire my work. "I'll take this out and then check on the kids."

"When I came in I saw Alex and Diego had most of the kids in the den. They set up a play area and it appeared the little ones were having a blast. Alex was supervising Catherine and Eli, who were playing with Harper and Morgan while Diego was entertaining the kids in the five-to-ten age range. Most of the older kids are in the pool." Hazel set the tray she'd filled aside and started on another. "It's so nice of you to throw this party for everyone year after year. I'm sure it's a lot of work."

"Ellie and Zak help. Levi too. And I enjoy it. Yes, it's a lot of work, but it wouldn't be Halloween without the Spooktacular. I'm going to start taking out what we have." I picked up a tray in each hand and headed to the dining room, where we'd set up a buffet table. The house was packed with people I loved, which should have made me happy, yet I still felt a little sad.

"Something wrong?" Nona asked.

I smiled. "No. I'm great. Are you having a good time?"

"I am. It's nice to be part of a family after so many years of being on my own. It's so nice of you and Zak to welcome me into your home the way you have."

"You know we're happy to have you here. Did your date arrive?"

Nona nodded. "See that handsome man talking to your dad? His name is Grover."

I looked toward the man, who had to be at least twenty years younger than Nona. I supposed that made him perfect in her eyes. "He looks familiar."

"He's a mechanic in town. He works on cars but specializes in hogs like mine. I like a man with grease under his fingernails. And he's a drummer in a rock band, which is an added bonus."

I placed a hand on Nona's arm. "He sounds great."

"He is, which is why we're going to take off for some alone time."

I glanced at the man again. He seemed like a nice enough guy, but I'd felt a bit protective of Nona since her brain surgery. "Should we expect you back this evening?"

Nona shrugged. "Don't wait up. I'm thinking I'll take my bike. Been a while since I took her for a ride."

I smiled. It looked like a bit of the old Nona was slowly returning. "Have fun, but be safe."

"Always."

I headed back to the kitchen for two more trays. I was glad Nona was getting her groove back, but I wasn't sure I was up for a full-blown, crazy Nona as a permanent houseguest. Maybe she'd settle into a happy medium, with just the right mix of crazy and settled.

******

I stood in the drive waving to Levi and Ellie, who had stayed late to help us clean up. The party had been a huge success, but I was exhausted. Zak walked up behind me and wrapped his arms around my waist, his breath warm on my neck. "I have a surprise for you," he whispered into my ear as the taillights faded.

I turned slightly. "Surprise? What kind of surprise?"

"Close your eyes."

I did as instructed. Zak took my hand and started to walk.

"Where are we going?" I asked as I struggled not to trip.

"You'll see. Be sure to keep your eyes closed."

I laughed. "I can't see where I'm going. The ground is uneven. I could very well end up flat on my face."

Zak stopped walking. "Hang on." The next thing I knew, I was being lifted into Zak's strong arms. I put my arms around his neck and hung on tight.

"Are your eyes still closed?" Zak asked as he walked with me hugged to his chest.

"They are. Where are we going?"

"You'll see. Just hang on for one more minute."

"You know you're crazy." I giggled.

"I know." Zak stopped walking. He turned slightly. "Okay, open your eyes."

I opened my eyes and gasped. Somehow, in the few short minutes between everyone leaving and now, Zak had turned the spa area into a Halloween fairyland. The indoor/outdoor roof and exterior wall had been retracted so the stars shone overhead. There was a fire in the fire pit, which provided the only illumination in the dark night other than the hundreds of orange lights that were strung overhead.

"How did you do all this?"

Zak slowly set me onto the ground in front of him. He handed me a glass of champagne. "Levi helped me while you and Ellie finished up in the kitchen."

"It's wonderful, but why?"

Zak kissed my neck. "Seemed like a good night for a spa for two under the stars."

I took a sip of my champagne and leaned against Zak's body behind me. "This is so totally perfect, but what about the kids?"

"All of them went to your parents' for an overnight stay."

"Really?" Suddenly I couldn't help but smile. "And Nona?"

"I booked her a suite in town. She knew she was staying there when she left with her guy friend, but I swore her to secrecy. Tonight it is all about you and me, a bottle of chilled champagne, a bubbly hot spa, and these totally awesome lights I strung overhead. Do you like it?"

My eyes teared up as I nodded. "I love it." God, how I loved this funny, thoughtful man I suddenly couldn't stop kissing.

Up next from Kathi Daley Books

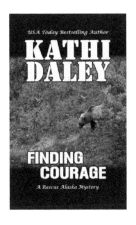

Preview Chapter 1

Saturday, October 13

His pulse quickened as they approached. He'd waited so long. Too long. He closed his eyes and reveled in the memory, which didn't come as a gentle wave but as a surge of agony from the depths of his personal hell. He'd craved the searing pain, the deeply felt anguish. It was only during these moments, when he was sure he would drown in a river of longing, that he felt truly alive.

On the surface, the rescue seemed fairly routine. Two teenage boys had gone hiking earlier that morning. They were only supposed to be gone a couple of hours but had failed to return by the time they'd agreed to meet with the families for lunch. The father of one of the boys had gone looking for them, and when he was unable to find them after a couple of hours, he'd called the Rescue Alaska Search and Rescue Team, of which I, Harmony Carson, am a member. It was fall in Alaska, which meant the days were becoming shorter toward the endless night of winter. Although the daytime temperatures were mild for this time of the year, the overnight low promised to dip well below freezing. Normally, we like to interview the person making the call, but the man said he was heading toward Devil's Gulch, where he was certain the boys had been planning to hike, and the reception there was sketchy, so the information we had to go on was limited. By the time the call came through, the sun had begun its descent toward the jagged peak of the distant mountain, so we knew there was no time to lose.

Jake Cartwright, my best friend and brother-in-law, had taken the call. I was already at Neverland, the bar Jake owns and where I work as a waitress, as was S&R team member Wyatt Forrester, who worked part time there as a bartender. Jake had made a quick decision to employ the team members present to look for the boys, so he and his S&R dog, Sitka, me and my S&R dog, Yukon, Wyatt, and team member Austin Brown, who happened to be in the bar having a drink, set off with a feeling of urgency, given the sharp drop in temperature and impending darkness.

"Jake to Harmony," Jake said over the two-way radio we all carried as we traveled toward our destination.

"Go for Harmony," I answered. We'd spread out to cover more ground in the event the boys had either doubled back or taken another route. We knew if we didn't find them before then, once we reached the narrow entrance to the gulch, we'd all converge into a single unit.

"Have you managed to pick up anything?" Jake referred to my ability to psychically connect to those victims I was meant to help rescue. My ability, which I oftentimes considered a curse, had come to me during the lowest point in my life. My sister Val, who had become my guardian after our parents were killed in an accident, had gone out on a rescue. She'd become lost in a storm, and although the team tried to find her, they came up with nothing but dead ends. She was the first person I connected to, and the one I most wanted to save. I couldn't save Val, but since then, I've used my gift to locate and rescue dozens of people. I couldn't save them all, but today, I was determined that our search would lead us to the missing boys.

"No," I answered, frustration evident in my voice. "Which is odd. Even if the boys are uninjured, they must be scared. The temperature has dropped and the sun is beginning to set. The fact that I'm not getting anything at all is concerning me."

There are really only three reasons I can think of when I don't pick up something, even a small whisper, during a rescue. The most common is that the person who's been reported missing isn't really missing at all. They might not have checked in with the person who reported them as missing, but they were perfectly safe, not in physical pain or mental duress. I hoped that would turn out to be the case with the two boys.

The second commonest reason I'm unable to pick up a psychic connection is because the person I'm trying to reach is either unconscious or already dead. That's the reason I least hope to confirm, but at times, the person we're trying to find has already taken his final breath before we even begin our search.

And the third reason I'm occasionally unable to make a connection is because the person in need of rescue senses me but is blocking me. This rarely occurs, but it's possible.

"Is Sitka picking up anything?" I asked. Even if I was unable to connect, I'd think Sitka would pick up something. We didn't have anything with the boys' scent to help direct the dogs today, so they'd been instructed to find anyone who might be in the area. Having a specific scent to track worked a lot better, but at this time of the year, when there weren't many people out hiking, if anyone was around, the dogs should be able to locate them.

"No. Nothing specific at least, but he does seem to sense someone," Jake answered. "If the boys came this way, as the father seemed to think they had, he'll find them. If they veered off in another direction, though, we might have a real problem. Given the anticipated overnight temps, it's important to find them as quickly as possible. We're going to go on, but I'd like you to take a short break and really try to connect. If you sense something, let us know."

"Okay." I stopped walking and looked around. "I don't have a lot to go on, but I'll try."

"The man I spoke to said the boys' names are Mark and Andrew. They're both fourteen and have dark hair and dark eyes. That's all I got from him before he cut out."

I signed off, then sat down on a large rock. I instructed to Yukon to sit and stay next to me, then I closed my eyes. I relaxed my mind and focused on the information I had. Mark and Andrew. Scared, most likely. Possibly injured. Dark hair, dark eyes.

Nothing. Absolutely nothing.

I tried again. I allowed whatever images that came to me to pass through my mind. I hoped if they were out there, their psyches would somehow find mine.

Still nothing.

I had an intuition that the man who'd called Jake to report the missing teens had been less than honest.

If I had to guess, this whole thing was a hoax. It happened from time to time, although I had no idea why anyone would do such a thing. Still, if the boys actually were in the area and were in some sort of trouble, it was likely I'd pick up an echo of fear if nothing else. I was about to give up my quest to make a connection and had stood up to move on when a feeling of sorrow pierced my heart with such intensity that it left me gasping for air.

Oh God. My hand clenched my chest.

My instinct was to break the connection, but I knew if I wanted to locate the source of the pain I needed to maintain it, so I took a deep breath and opened my heart to the anguish. I allowed the pain to envelop me as I tried to figure out who it was I'd connected to. I could sense the distress was emotional rather than physical. Someone was dealing with intense grief. No, not grief, longing. The suffering was deep and real, but there was something else as well. I frowned. In the midst of the sorrow was anticipation.

I focused harder. I knew I hadn't connected to the boys but someone else. Someone older. I could sense a darkness. An emptiness. As if the soul of the person I'd connected with had been drained of all life. I felt the individual try to pull back. He knew I'd made a connection and was trying to push me away, but I resisted. I tried to go deeper, but then I saw it. My eyes flew open.

My hand flew to my mouth. I was sure I was going to be sick, but I thrust the nausea aside. "Harmony to Jake."

"Go for Jake."

"It's a trap. Pull back. Pull back now."

In that instant, there was a loud crash as the mountain above the narrow opening to the gulch exploded, sending tons of dirt and rock to the path below. I turned and ran as fast as I could. Tears streamed down my face, but I didn't really notice. I felt fear, and pain, and death.

Oh God.

I ran faster still. Yukon was running in front of me. He must have sensed where to go because he never wavered. When I arrived at the place where the dirt and rock had settled, I found Sitka standing over Jake, who appeared to be unconscious.

"Jake." I ran to where he was laying on the hard ground and felt for a pulse. I let out a breath of relief when I saw he had one. He had a bump on his head but appeared to be otherwise uninjured. I grabbed my radio and called Sarge, who was holding down the fort at base. "Harmony to Sarge."

"Go for Sarge."

"There's been an accident. A landslide. Find Jordan. Have her meet Dani at the helipad. We're going to need an air evacuation. And Sarge, tell them to hurry."

With that, I stood up and slowly looked around. I wasn't sure where Austin and Wyatt were. Had they been with Jake? In front of him? On another trail altogether?

I heard Jake groan. I turned to find both Sitka and Yukon licking his face. I knelt down next to him. "Are you okay?"

Jake put his hand to his head. "What happened?"

"Landslide. You were hit in the head with something. You blacked out but appear to be otherwise okay. Where were Wyatt and Austin before the mountain came down?"

Jake sat up. His face paled. "In front of me."

I looked down at Sitka and Yukon. "Find Wyatt. Find Austin."

The dogs ran on ahead, and I knew I needed to follow, but the dizziness and nausea I'd kept at bay had returned. I was fine, I reminded myself. I'd seen something I'd need to process, but the most important thing was to find my friends. I stood up and looked at the spot in front of me, where the trail had once been. This was bad. Really bad.

It didn't take the dogs long to find Wyatt. He'd managed to find a place next to the wall of the canyon to crouch down, avoiding most of the debris from above. After a bit of back and forth, we determined he was trapped and hurt. Jake managed to get up despite his head injury to help me dig him out. It was a long, arduous process because each rock needed to be lifted and set aside. I don't know how we found the strength to do it, but when I saw Wyatt's face, bruised but alert, I wanted to cry in relief.

His leg was broken and his shoulder dislocated but he didn't appear to have any life-threatening injuries. By the time Jake and I had freed him, the sun had set, but we could hear Dani's chopper in the distance. I wasn't sure I had any strength left, but we weren't done. "Find Austin," I said to the dogs, even though I suspected he was gone. I'd been able to sense Wyatt as the dogs looked for him, but when I focused on Austin, all I found was silence. Of course, if he was unconscious I might not be able to make a connection, so there was the hope for me to cling to. I tried to keep up as the dogs scrambled over the rubble. Wyatt hadn't been all that far in front of Jake and so hadn't been in the area of largest destruction, but the farther toward the center of the landslide the dogs traveled, the more certain I was Austin was gone. By the time Dani had landed the chopper, Sitka alerted. He'd found Austin.

Sometimes all you can do is what you have to do. Dani had brought both Jordan and Sarge with her, so they helped load Wyatt into the chopper, where Jordan went to work on his injuries. Once Wyatt was in Jordan's hands, Dani and Sarge helped us retrieve Austin's body. By the time we'd freed him from the rubble, it was completely dark and the temperature had dropped at least thirty degrees. Jake was still dizzy from his head injury, and we couldn't all fit in the chopper at the same time, so Jordan went with Dani, who flew Wyatt and Jake to the hospital, while Sarge waited with the dogs and me. Austin's body would be airlifted down as well, but it was more important to see to the injured.

"It wasn't an accident," I said to Sarge after we'd built a fire for warmth, then settled in to wait for Dani to come back for us.

"What do you mean, it wasn't an accident?"

I tilted my head up so I could more clearly see the northern lights overhead. I wanted to embrace the breathtaking beauty that could be found in the Alaskan wilderness, but all I could feel was grief. "In the brief moment before the mountain exploded, I connected with someone in so much pain it was almost unbearable. I felt the rawness of exposed emotion as grief was channeled into rage." I lowered my head and looked at Sarge. "Someone lured us up here. Someone set off explosives and intentionally caused the landslide. I have no doubt the intention was to bury us all, but I'd stopped to try to make a connection, so I was well behind the others. When I realized what was happening, I was able to warn Jake, which gave him maybe a second to retreat." I swallowed as a lump of emotion clogged my throat. "Jake told me that he'd called to the others, but the mountain was already coming down and they were too far ahead."

Sarge was silent for a moment. I imagined he needed that time to try to process what I'd just said. To lose a member of the team to a random landslide was bad enough; to lose him to a madman was another thing entirely. "So you're saying Austin was murdered."

I nodded. "Yes. I'm saying that." I took a deep breath as my entire body began to shake.

"Are you okay?" Sarge looked me in the eye. He put his hands on my shoulders and gave me a little shake.

"I'm okay. It's just that..." I couldn't continue. I tried to speak, but at that moment I couldn't even breathe. I felt my heart pounding in my chest as a flash of memory seared through my mind.

"Just that what?" Sarge said persuasively. "You didn't finish what you were saying."

I shook my head. I couldn't speak. I didn't want to remember.

"You know you can trust me."

I nodded. Sitka and Yukon were sitting so close to me, they were practically in my lap. I could sense their distress. I needed to pull myself together, but I wasn't sure how I was going to do that.

"I want to help you, but you need to finish your thought," Sarge insisted.

I put my arms around the dogs and took comfort in their warmth. I let them lick the tears from my face, and then I answered. Softly at first, but as my voice found its footing, I went on with more intensity. "In that moment, when I connected to whoever set off the dynamite that caused the landslide, I saw something else. A memory. Not my memory, *his* memory."

Sarge frowned. "Okay. What was it?"

"It was Val." I felt my body begin to shake again. "He was with her. The man who killed Austin was with Val when she died."

Recipes

Spinach Tortellini Soup—submitted by Sharon Guagliardo
Sauce Pot Meatballs—submitted by Vivian Shane
Chuck Wagon Casserole—submitted by Patty Liu
Chicken Divan—submitted by Joyce Aiken

Spinach Tortellini Soup

Submitted by Sharon Guagliardo

This is another recipe we enjoyed from a friend.

2 cloves garlic, chopped fine
1 tbs. butter
2 cans chicken broth (College Inn)
16-oz. can stewed tomatoes, chopped
1 pkg. fresh or frozen cheese-filled tortellini
1 pkg. frozen spinach drained or 1 pkg. fresh, cleaned and chopped

Sauté garlic in butter. Add chicken broth and tomatoes. Bring to boil; add tortellini and spinach. Simmer until tortellini is done.

Meanwhile, prepare basil-parmesan topping (below).

Season soup to taste with salt and pepper. Ladle into large soup bowls, drizzle on olive oil, and generously sprinkle with a tbs. or two of the topping.

Top each serving with a little Parmesan cheese and serve with garlic bread and a nice tossed salad.

Serves 6 to 8

Basil-parmesan topping:

¾ cup freshly grated imported Parmesan cheese
¼ cup finely chopped fresh basil leaves
Coarsely ground black pepper to taste

Blend Parmesan cheese, fresh basil, and pepper in a small bowl. Use as garnish.

Note: I add a package of frozen meatballs, quartered, along with the broth and tomatoes.

Sauce Pot Meatballs

Submitted by Vivian Shane

One of my favorite oldie-but-goodie recipes. Most of the time it's just my husband and myself, so I like recipes you cook once and eat twice! I make spaghetti and meatballs one day and then meatball sandwiches the next with the leftovers.

1 pkg dry onion soup mix
1¼ cups water
2 8-oz. cans tomato sauce
1 lbs. ground beef
½ tsp. garlic salt
¼ tsp. thyme
¼ tsp. pepper
1 tbs. parsley

In a deep saucepan, bring to a boil the onion soup mix, water, and 1½ cups tomato sauce. Simmer, covered, for 10 minutes. Mix ground beef, seasonings, parsley, and remaining tomato sauce. Shape into 16 meatballs and gently place in sauce. Simmer uncovered for 25 minutes, turning occasionally.

Chuck Wagon Casserole

Submitted by Patty Liu

1 lbs. lean ground beef
½ large onion, chopped
1 green bell pepper, medium-size, chopped
1 tsp. garlic salt
1 tbs. chili powder
1 can diced tomatoes, undrained
1 can kidney beans, drained
1 large can whole-kernel corn, drained
Pinch of ground cumin
1 tbs. Worcestershire sauce
Hot red pepper sauce to taste
Salt and pepper to taste
1 cup shredded cheddar cheese

Preheat oven to 350 degrees. Spray a 2-qt. casserole dish with Pam Original. In a large skillet, brown meat until lightly browned. Add onion, bell pepper, garlic salt, and chili powder; stir till vegetables are softened. Scrape mixture into casserole dish; add tomatoes, beans, com, cumin, and Worcestershire sauce. Season with hot sauce, salt, and pepper, stir well, and bake uncovered 30 minutes. Sprinkle cheese over top and continue to bake until top is golden brown, about 20 minutes.

Serves 6 to 8

Chicken Divan

Submitted by Joyce Aiken

A good friend brought this to me when I had surgery nine years ago. She makes it for potluck suppers at her church and for her husband's birthday every year, and they love it. We love it too!

2 cans cream of chicken soup
½ cup Miracle Whip + a small amount of milk
16-oz. bag frozen broccoli, thawed but not cooked
4 chicken breasts, roasted, then chilled and cut into cubes
1 cup shredded cheddar cheese
½ cup bread crumbs
3 tbs. melted butter

 Mix soup and Miracle Whip and add small amount of milk to make it pourable.

Spray a 9x13-inch pan with Pam. Layer in this order, using all of each item once:
broccoli on the bottom of the pan
cubed chicken
soup/Miracle Whip/milk mixture
sprinkle with cheddar cheese
sprinkle with bread crumbs
drizzle butter over all

Bake at 350 degrees for 45 minutes or until bubbly. You can cut this recipe in half and use an 8 x 8 pan. Don't freeze leftovers because of the Miracle Whip.

Books by Kathi Daley

Come for the murder, stay for the romance

Zoe Donovan Cozy Mystery:
Halloween Hijinks
The Trouble With Turkeys
Christmas Crazy
Cupid's Curse
Big Bunny Bump-off
Beach Blanket Barbie
Maui Madness
Derby Divas
Haunted Hamlet
Turkeys, Tuxes, and Tabbies
Christmas Cozy
Alaskan Alliance
Matrimony Meltdown
Soul Surrender
Heavenly Honeymoon
Hopscotch Homicide
Ghostly Graveyard
Santa Sleuth
Shamrock Shenanigans
Kitten Kaboodle
Costume Catastrophe
Candy Cane Caper
Holiday Hangover
Easter Escapade
Camp Carter
Trick or Treason
Reindeer Roundup
Hippity Hoppity Homicide

Firework Fiasco
Henderson House
Holiday Heist – *January 2019*

Zimmerman Academy The New Normal
Ashton Falls Cozy Cookbook

Tj Jensen Paradise Lake Mysteries by Henery Press:

Pumpkins in Paradise
Snowmen in Paradise
Bikinis in Paradise
Christmas in Paradise
Puppies in Paradise
Halloween in Paradise
Treasure in Paradise
Fireworks in Paradise
Beaches in Paradise

Rescue Alaska Paranormal Mystery:
Finding Justice
Finding Answers
Finding Courage - *September 2018*
Finding Christmas – *December 2018*

Whales and Tails Cozy Mystery:

Romeow and Juliet
The Mad Catter
Grimm's Furry Tail
Much Ado About Felines
Legend of Tabby Hollow
Cat of Christmas Past
A Tale of Two Tabbies
The Great Catsby
Count Catula
The Cat of Christmas Present
A Winter's Tail
The Taming of the Tabby
Frankencat
The Cat of Christmas Future
Farewell to Felines
A Whisker in Time – *September 2018*
The Catsgiving Feast – *November 2018*

Writers' Retreat Mystery:

First Case
Second Look
Third Strike
Fourth Victim
Fifth Night
Sixth Cabin
Seventh Chapter

A Tess and Tilly Mystery:

The Christmas Letter
The Valentine Mystery
The Mother's Day Mishap
The Halloween House

The Thanksgiving Trip – *October 2018*

Haunting by the Sea:
Homecoming by the Sea
Secrets by the Sea
Missing by the Sea – *October 2018*
Christmas by the Sea – *December 2018*

Sand and Sea Hawaiian Mystery:
Murder at Dolphin Bay
Murder at Sunrise Beach
Murder at the Witching Hour
Murder at Christmas
Murder at Turtle Cove
Murder at Water's Edge
Murder at Midnight

Seacliff High Mystery:
The Secret
The Curse
The Relic
The Conspiracy
The Grudge
The Shadow
The Haunting

Road to Christmas Romance:
Road to Christmas Past

USA Today best-selling author Kathi Daley lives in beautiful Lake Tahoe with her husband Ken. When she isn't writing, she likes spending time hiking the miles of desolate trails surrounding her home. She has authored more than seventy-five books in eight series, including Zoe Donovan Cozy Mysteries, Whales and Tails Island Mysteries, Sand and Sea Hawaiian Mysteries, Tj Jensen Paradise Lake Series, Writers' Retreat Southern Seashore Mysteries, Rescue Alaska Paranormal Mysteries, and Seacliff High Teen Mysteries. Find out more about her books at **www.kathidaley.com**

Stay up-to-date:

Newsletter, *The Daley Weekly*
http://eepurl.com/NRPDf
Webpage – **www.kathidaley.com**
Facebook at Kathi Daley Books –
www.facebook.com/kathidaleybooks
Kathi Daley Books Group Page –
https://www.facebook.com/groups/569578823146850/
E-mail – **kathidaley@kathidaley.com**
Twitter at Kathi Daley@kathidaley –
https://twitter.com/kathidaley
Amazon Author Page –
https://www.amazon.com/author/kathidaley
BookBub –
https://www.bookbub.com/authors/kathi-daley

CPSIA information can be obtained
at www.ICGtesting.com
Printed in the USA
LVHW081317180321
681855LV00027B/533